Teaching Handbook

Y3/P4

Maureen Lewis

Series Editor

OXFORD

Project X Creative Team

Series Editor: Maureen Lewis

Series Consultants: Christine Cork (Primary Strategy Consultant, Kent) and Pippa Doran (Senior English Advisor, Kent)

Scottish Consultants: Louise Ballantyne (Project Manager Literacy, LTS) and Sue Ellis (University of Strathclyde)

Lead Author: (character books): Tony Bradman

Illustrator: (character books): Jon Stuart, Jonatronix Ltd

***Guided/Group Reading Notes* author team:** Maureen Lewis, Jo Tregenza, Amanda Snowden, Sue Huxley, Anne Derry, Katie Frost

Project X concept by Rod Theodorou and Emma Lynch

The publisher wishes to thank the following schools for their valuable contribution to the trialling and development of Project X:

Hawkedon Primary School, Reading; Bordesley Green Primary School, Birmingham; Witton Gilbert Primary School, Durham; St Patricks RC VA Primary School, Consett; St Andrew's CE Primary School, Rochdale; Temple Primary School, Manchester; West Denton First School, Newcastle Upon Tyne; Wardley Primary School, Gateshead; New Hinksey CE Primary School, Oxford; New Marston Primary School, Oxford; St Andrews CE Primary School, Oxford; Sunningwell CE Primary School, Abingdon; St Nicolas CE Primary School, Abingdon; Lee Mount Primary School, Halifax; Long Wittenham CE Primary School, Abingdon; Charlton On Otmoor Primary School, Oxford; Carnmoney Primary School, County Antrim; Stracathro Primary School, Angus; James Gillespie Primary School, Edinburgh; Malcolm Primary School, London; Sherborne CE Primary School, Cheltenham

OXFORD
UNIVERSITY PRESS

is a department of the University of Oxford.
It furthers the University's objective of excellence in research, scholarship,
and education by publishing worldwide.

Text and illustrations © Oxford University Press 2009

Acknowledgements
The publisher would like to thank the following for permission to reproduce photographs:
p12t Tony Bradman; **p12**b Jon Stuart, **p14b** OUP/photodisk; **p62** Monkey Business Images/Shutterstock; All other photography © OUP/ MTJ Media.

Photocopy masters Illustrations by Michael Garton

First published in 2009

Project X concept by Rod Theodorou and Emma Lynch

ISBN: 978-0-19-847011-3

1 3 5 7 9 10 8 6 4 2

Printed in Great Britain by Printed in Great Britain by Bell & Bain

Paper used in the production of this book is a natural, recyclable product made
from wood grown in sustainable forests. The manufacturing process conforms
to the environmental regulations of the country of origin.

Contents

Project X – Structure and components

Year Group	Book Band	ORT Stage	Cluster Packs – five books linked by a theme, plus guided/group reading notes
Reception /P1	1	1+	
	2	2	
	3	3	
Year 1/P2	4	4	
	5	5	
	6	6	
Year 2/P3	7	7	
	8	8	
	9	9	
	10	10	
	11	11	
Year 3/P4	11	11	
	12	10 11	
Year 4/P5	13	12 13	

Teachers' Resources		Interactive Resources
Teaching Handbook		6 stories to read and explore
Teaching Handbook		6 stories to read and explore
Teaching Handbook	Project X Handbook: Raising Reading Achievement for Boys • Proven strategies for getting boys reading • Practical advice to help you make it happen Girls will benefit, too!	6 stories to read and explore
Teaching Handbook		6 stories to read and explore
Teaching Handbook		

Welcome to Project X!

Project X is a an innovative new reading programme designed to hook young children in to reading in Reception/P1, support them in their early reading development, and turn them into confident, independent and enthusiastic readers by the time they reach Year 4/P5.

The series of 140 stunning and highly original books offers an interesting, exciting and motivating choice of reading materials for 21st century children. These include top quality stories by some of the very best writers for children, fascinating information books, and electronic texts supported by audio and visual media. Whilst designed to appeal to all children, the books give special attention to the needs and tastes of boy readers – a benefit outlined in more detail on pages 7–9.

Motivation is crucial to the success of most readers, particularly boys. For this reason, the teaching and learning approaches underpinning **Project X** emphasize the importance of comprehension and engagement in learning to read. The books have been developed, first and foremost, to be *great reads*, although the importance of developing decoding and word recognition skills in the early stages of reading is not overlooked. The action-packed stories and fascinating non-fiction material provide ample opportunities for children to apply and reinforce their decoding skills, in line with the pace and progression in phonics recommended by *Letters and Sounds*.

What makes Project X different?

- **Project X** is a new generation guided reading programme especially designed to appeal to boys and to help raise reading standards for all your pupils.
- It is **truly boy-friendly** in its content, design, structure, and teaching and learning approach.
- It contains an **amazing new character adventure** that will hook children in to reading and keep them reading.
- It offers **unique thematic clusters** of books on topics that children will love – great for motivation, supporting progress and linking to the wider curriculum.
- It offers **exceptional support for guided reading**, with easy to use notes and advice on assessment for learning.
- It is the **perfect complement to your existing resources** – Book Banded and linked to Oxford Reading Tree stages.

Project X – Turning boys into real readers

Project X has been created to meet the needs and interests of all children. However, there is a wealth of research showing that there are specific challenges involved in ensuring some boys become readers. Boys are more likely than girls to struggle with reading and to give up on independent reading. Boys are also far more likely than girls to under perform in writing. In the *Rose Review* of March 2006, Jim Rose identified: "urgent concerns about the generally weaker performance of boys than girls".

For these reasons **Project X** has been designed to include content and elements of teaching and learning practice which will particularly support boys while not disadvantaging girls.

Research also shows that in schools where there is little or no achievement gap between girls and boys, teachers:

- have high expectations of all the children in the class
- avoid gender or other stereotyping
- use an active teaching style
- try to get all children involved
- make use of formative assessment.

Project X supports teachers in embedding such approaches into their practice.

Why do boys struggle with reading?

The reasons for some boys' underperformance in literacy are complex and often include wider societal factors such as gender roles and stereotypes, family influences, behaviour issues, peer pressure and self-stereotyping. There are also factors relating directly to the teaching of reading such as boys' early reading experiences, teacher expectations, teaching and learning practices, learning contexts and book choice. One factor, however, stands out above all others when it comes to boys and learning and that is *motivation*. When it comes to reading and writing boys, far more than girls, need to see a clear purpose for what they are doing. They won't simply do something because they are told to; they want to know what's in it for them. For some boys it is not that they can't, it is just that they can't be bothered!

As well as motivating content, a number of teaching and learning practices have been shown to be successful in addressing gender issues in school and in supporting boy readers. All of these have been incorporated into **Project X**.

● Book choice and content

The **Project X** books reflect the genres that we know boys love, whilst offering a good range of materials to broaden their reading experiences. The stories, written mostly by male authors, are fast-paced and full of action, adventure, humour and fantasy and the emphasis on character is guaranteed to hook readers in. The design of some of the books includes those 'comic book' conventions, such as visual literacy, so popular with boys. The non-fiction book topics have been chosen specifically to appeal to boy readers and to be both interesting and challenging.

Social identity

Readers can confirm and extend their own identity through reading and so build their confidence and engagement. The core characters in **Project X** think, act and feel in ways that modern children, particularly boys, will be able to relate to. However they do not represent gender stereotypes. They show both active and affective aspects of identity. The non-fiction books present inspirational role models and include content that emphasizes teamwork, dealing with difficult emotions, individual endeavour and people facing the challenges of everyday life.

The importance of talk

Discussing and reflecting on books is a vital part of becoming an engaged reader and talking to gather ideas is an important strategy for becoming a writer. Boys in particular benefit from articulating and reinforcing their thoughts and ideas through talk. The **Project X** books have been developed to offer a wealth of discussion opportunities, and speaking and listening strategies and activities are embedded throughout the teaching support.

Experiential, creative and reflective follow-up activities

Boys – and in fact most young learners – tend to prefer active and experiential ways of learning to sitting still and being silent! The teaching ideas provided with each **Project X** book include suggestions for physical experiences to support active learning. The wide range of literacy and cross-curricular follow-up activities include many ideas for interactive teaching and learning and address a range of teaching and learning styles – aural, visual, kinaesthetic.

Regular reviews of progress and target setting

Boys like to have clear learning targets in order to understand their reason for learning. They also like to see evidence of their progress as they find achievement and recognition motivating. Each guided/group reading session provided in the **Project X** teaching notes has a clear focus – with targets and assessment criteria that can be used for regular learning reviews. There are also peer and self assessment sheets for children to record their progress (see pages 47-50).

ICT and multimedia literacy

Today's children are growing up in a multimedia world. As well as being highly engaging and motivating for children, films, cartoons, websites, computer games and other multimedia texts often present specific and sophisticated literacy challenges. It is important that pupils' experience in using such forms of literacy is acknowledged, appreciated and developed if they are to be fully literate in the 21st century.

Project X responds to this in two ways. Firstly, the series aims to engage young readers by using a detailed, 3D digital illustration style for the character books. This brings the world of films and computer games to books and has been a huge hit with children in our trials. Secondly, **Project X** offers a collection of stories on screen that include audio, animation and video elements to engage children, stimulate discussion and support both traditional and multimedia literacy skills.

Family involvement

Building a reading culture at home as well as in school is important so that boys see reading as something to engage with beyond the school environment. Involving fathers or other males in reading with boys has been shown to be successful in encouraging this. Some specific advice on involving parents in their children's reading is given in this handbook (see pages 62–63) and each of the **Project X** books contains some simple questions and activities to support parents/carers in reading with their children.

Reading role models

It is important for boys to see others, particularly other males, reading. This reinforces the place that reading has in society. Some of the **Project X** stories have purposeful uses of literacy woven in to the plot and the core characters – Max, Cat, Ant and Tiger – are often shown reading and writing for different purposes.

Competitive approaches

Much of the research into raising boys' achievement shows that competitive approaches to learning can be effective. This doesn't mean setting children against each other but against their own personal targets. On pages 47-50 you will find self-assessment sheets for each level of the **Project X** books in Year 3/P4 and these can be used to help children track their own progress against their reading targets.

Celebration of achievement

Ongoing praise, together with recognition and reward for success are vitally important to young learners, particularly boys. On pages 54–55 of this Handbook you will find reading and writing certificates templates that can be used to celebrate achievement.

What about the girls?

It is important to state that **Project X** is not just about boys. Girls too benefit from the kinds of teaching and learning outlined above. Additionally, almost all of the evidence from research, case studies and various Raising Boys' Achievement initiatives that fed in to the development of **Project X** shows that if you can engage boys with reading there are huge benefits for girls. Classroom reality often means that disengaged boys take up disproportionately more teacher time and that quiet, well-behaved, often middle ability girls suffer as a result. Engaged boys give teachers more time to ensure that every child is being helped to progress at the right pace. Girls can also benefit from the lively and imaginative discussion that engaged boys participate in – improving their comprehension skills and the quality of their writing.

In terms of content and book choice, girls are generally open to exploring a wide range of texts whilst boys are much more likely to have a narrower range of preferences. So whilst the **Project X** books have been developed to appeal to boys there is no reason why girls won't love them too! The character strand of **Project X** includes a strong girl character in Cat, an adult female heroine in the shape of Dani Day, and explores themes such as family and friendship that are traditionally seen to be appealing to girls.

> The *Raising the Reading Achievement of Boys* book that accompanies **Project X** gives more detailed information, advice and ideas for raising reading standards across your school.
> *Visit our website for details: www.OxfordPrimary.co.uk/projectx*

The Project X character books

Today's young children love **characters**. Almost all children's popular culture – from books to toys to TV to computer games – revolves around distinctive characters. Some are enduring favourites, like Spiderman, Scooby Doo, Postman Pat and Thomas the Tank Engine, but there are new characters being created all the time – Peppa Pig, Ben 10, Power Rangers … the list is endless.

Following the adventures of well-loved characters is widely acknowledged as one of the best ways to hook young children in to reading … and to keep them reading. At the heart of **Project X** lies a group of exciting new characters.

Meet the characters

Project X follows the adventures of Max, Cat, Ant and Tiger – four children who one day discover four amazing watches that allow them to shrink. They have many fantastic and action-packed micro-adventures, exploring an ordinary world made extraordinary by their micro-size. It is a world in which they have power and independence, solve their own problems and gradually form strong, though often tested, bonds of friendship. The four children (three boys, one girl) have personalities and habits that today's children will be able to relate to, whilst providing positive role models for readers.

Max

As the series progresses, the adventures evolve into episodes within an overarching 'soap' style story. The books can be read in any order and not all books have to be read, but in the background an exciting master plot is developing that readers from Year 2/P3 upwards will gradually uncover.

Within each thematic cluster of books in the series, there is also a non-fiction book featuring one or more of the characters as 'guides' who pose questions, reflect thoughts and make comment on the content. The use of character in a non-fiction context helps to engage the reader with the content and makes the books more interactive.

Cat

The character story in Year 3/P4

In Reception/P1 and Year 1/P2, the character story books feature a series of micro-adventures in familiar settings such as home, garden, park and school. Each book stands alone as a simple – yet amazing – micro-adventure. The four characters, their watches and their shrinking powers are introduced and developed so that the formula of the character strand becomes familiar.

Ant

In Year 2/P3 readers discover more about the origins of the four watches. There are hints of a mysterious creator and little spy robots begin to appear. The micro-adventures become more sophisticated and take our characters beyond the familiar locations and situations of the early levels.

Tiger

In Year 3/P4 – or from Lime Band upwards – readers gradually discover the truth about the watches and where they came from. They find out about the arch villain who created the watches – Dr X – and who desperately wants them back. In these stories Max, Cat, Ant and Tiger find themselves faced with a growing threat from Dr X's X-bots and must do battle with them to keep their watches safe. They meet Dani Day, the mysterious female scientist who will become a vital member of their team. Dr X's comic henchmen, Plug and Socket, appear in more stories and their incompetence provides a humorous contrast to the growing menace of the X-bots.

As well as the developing macro plot, Max, Cat, Ant and Tiger continue to have other micro-adventures which require them to be inventive and resourceful. The relationships within the group and individual personalities continue to develop, giving greater insight into their characters.

Although the books can be read in any order, and it is not expected that every child will read every book, there are certain 'key' books at Brown band in Year 3/P4 which, if read, will add to children's understanding and enjoyment of the overarching plot.

The Chase – by Anthony McGowan
(Brown band, Fast and Furious cluster)

In this book an X-bot succeeds in taking Tiger's watch – he must get it back! Max and Ant shrink and set off down the drains in pursuit of the X-bot while Cat uses the micro-copter to track the chase from the air. Tiger, unable to shrink, follows on his skateboard. As Max and Ant confront the many dangers concealed in the drains, the four friends must work together to retrieve Tiger's watch and save the day.

Heroine in Hiding – by Tony Bradman
(Brown band, Fast and Furious cluster)

In this story readers discover how Dani Day, a young female scientist employed by NICE, came to be working for Dr X and his NASTI organization. The story follows Dani as she learns about the power of the watches and Dr X's plans to shrink the world. Horrified, she decides to smuggle the watches out of NASTI headquarters – but not before she takes one watch for herself, shrinks down and goes in to hiding to keep an eye on Dr X. From her hiding place she sees Dr X create various X-bots designed to help him get his watches back.
She also discovers that four children have the watches. So Dani escapes in an X-pod on a bold mission to find the children and warn them of the gathering danger.

The X-bots are Coming ... – by Anthony McGowan
(Brown band, Strong Defences cluster)

Warned by Dani Day, the children know they must move from their den to a safer location and prepare for an X-bot attack. Taking an old toy fort on to an island in the pond in the park, the micro-friends prepare a set of defences that they hope will fend off their enemies. But as they successfully fight off the X2 robots, a sinister army of X3-bots gathers for a bigger attack ...

The Attack of the X-bots – by Anthony McGowan
(Brown band, Strong Defences cluster)

The X3 army reveal their increased powers as they launch an attack on the fort. A desperate battle ensues and although they use all their ingenuity and bravery the children's defences are gradually overcome. Max, Ant and Tiger watch as, in their moment of greatest peril, Cat runs away ... or does she?

To be continued ...

In Year 4/P5 – or at Grey band – the overarching story reaches its climax as Max, Cat, Ant and Tiger, with the help of Dani Day, have a final showdown with Dr X.

Dr X is a typical 'comic book' style villain – with typically dozy henchmen at his side. The stories of the children's battle to save the world from Dr X are action-packed, full of drama and strong on humour. They are designed to keep even the most reluctant child hooked in to reading, so that readers who can read don't become readers who won't read.

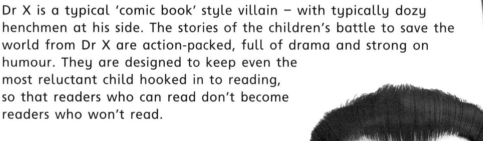

Creating the Project X character books

Max, Cat, Ant and Tiger are recognizable 21st century children and they are created on the page using modern, 3D computer-generated graphics. This gives them 'eye appeal' to children used to such sophisticated artwork from their very earliest years. This up-to-the minute design is coupled with texts written by the some of the very best children's authors.

The author team

The characters and the overarching story were created with the help of Tony Bradman – an experienced writer and editor of stories for children of all ages, best known for his *Dilly the Dinosaur* series. Through his writing and his many school visits and workshops, Tony brings to the series a passion for character and story and a genuine understanding of young readers' needs.

A core team of top quality writers – including Chris Powling, Anthony McGowan, Jan Burchett, Sara Vogler and Shoo Rayner – have worked alongside Tony on the character stories. Their challenge has been to maintain the continuity of character and plot whilst injecting a range of story ideas and writing styles to the series.

The illustrator

The stunning 3D illustrations created for **Project X** are the work of talented artist Jon Stuart and his team at Jonatronix Ltd. The artwork has involved the creation of thousands of character poses, props, settings and other amazing objects.

Each of the core characters is developed on a wire frame, allowing them to be moved, posed and positioned in the illustrations. Each character's face is made up of hundreds of 'virtual muscles', enabling us to create a range of detailed and authentic expressions.

Our illustrator works on a virtual film set, manipulating the characters and props and using a variety of textures and lighting techniques to create the stunning images you will see in the character books.

Project X brings the world of 3D animation and computer graphics to a reading programme for the very first time and is guaranteed to appeal to today's children!

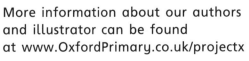

More information about our authors and illustrator can be found at www.OxfordPrimary.co.uk/projectx

Learning to read with Project X

Teachers want all their pupils to learn to read. They also want them to become effective and enthusiastic readers who understand what they read and recognize both the pleasure and usefulness of reading. The **Project X** programme shares these aims. Research shows there are several important factors in helping children become successful readers who understand what they read and who enjoy reading. **Project X** draws on this research which emphasizes the importance of the following factors:

Speaking and listening

Children's oral language and their ability to listen to others are crucial to the development of thinking and communication skills and underpin much of their learning, including learning to read.

Children first develop their understanding about the sounds, rhythms and structures of words and texts through listening to and by creating their own spoken texts. Listening to texts being read aloud or engaging in dialogue about texts helps build a varied oral vocabulary which in turn impacts on learning to read.

Children can also extend their engagement with texts by discussing them and elaborating on them through drama and role play. Talking about texts and orally questioning texts supports the development of comprehension – and with understanding comes the motivation to read more. Talk also helps children to gather ideas for writing.

Supporting children to develop and extend the vital skills of speaking and listening is embedded in **Project X** through a range of imaginative suggestions for purposeful and contextualized speaking and listening, group interaction and drama activities.

Project X recognizes that children come to school with a range of language skills and life experiences. Children for whom English is an additional language, for example, may be fluent in their first language but at an early stage in the development of their English. The **Project X** books and software provide content to prompt discussion that will broaden children's contextual and linguistic knowledge and in turn support their understanding of a text. For example, many of the **Project X** stories open with an information page, designed to set the context for the story. They may end with a story map to stimulate recall and retelling. The thematic 'cluster' structure of the programme broadens children's knowledge and understanding and offers lots of opportunities for discussion and comparison.

Reading strategies

Decoding/encoding and word recognition

Project X is not primarily a phonics programme but it does recognize and support the role of phonics and decoding skills in the early stages of learning to read. By Y3/P4 the majority of children will have moved on from needing to use phonics to decode as they read. Many words will be recognized on sight and children's reading fluency will continue to increase the more they read. Occasionally they may still call on their phonic knowledge when they encounter a new word, splitting multisyllabic words into syllables or words within words, to decode the sections they don't recognize. Phonic knowledge remains helpful for encoding in spelling and suggestions for spelling patterns to be found in the books are given in the *Guided/Group Reading Notes*.

The cluster structure of the books provides opportunities for revisiting and reinforcing vocabulary, particularly new or more challenging context words. Building vocabulary knowledge remains important for increasing reading fluency and comprehension so new vocabulary is often repeated within a text and across texts.

Context and syntactic clues

Decoding is one way of working out new words but readers also use a range of other strategies when approaching an unknown word, especially one that is not phonetically regular. Other strategies are also needed to understand the meaning of words. These cues continue to be important as the need for frequent decoding diminishes.

In using syntactic cues children use their implicit grammatical knowledge to identify the kind of word likely to be in the sentence (and to reject the kind of word unlikely to be there). The missing word in 'The cat _ _ _ on the mat' is likely to be a verb such as lay, sat, slept and so on. It is unlikely to be words such as blue (adjective) or under (preposition).

In using context cues children draw on their understanding of the meaning so far and their knowledge beyond the text to identify likely and unlikely words. 'The girl splashed in the pu_ _ _ _' is more likely to be puddle than pudding, for example. Readers will also use the supporting images to help them work out new words or to clarify their understanding.

Using these cues is not encouraging children to 'guess' words. Rather, they encourage children to use logic, prior knowledge and linguistic knowledge to help them narrow the range of possibilities and then use comprehension to check whether the word makes sense in the text.

How and when to use these approaches, by rereading a sentence, or monitoring for when a word makes sense but doesn't look right (reading said for shouted, for example) can be demonstrated by the teacher during shared reading. Children can then be encouraged to apply the strategies appropriately during guided and independent reading.

Comprehension

Building children's comprehension skills is given a high priority in **Project X**. Understanding what has been read is central to being an effective reader. Through making meaning within a text children become actively engaged with the text and can relate the text to their own world and life experiences, or extend these. If a child does not understand what they have read – even if they can segment and blend or recognize the words – they are unlikely to enjoy reading it.

Comprehension is not something that comes automatically. The latest research shows that children can be helped to develop comprehension skills by the explicit teaching of certain aspects of comprehension and by offering children specific strategies to help build these aspects. **Project X** helps teachers to recognize the opportunities within each book to focus on specific aspects of comprehension. Learning strategies to support these aspects of comprehension are given. Over time children develop a repertoire of comprehension strategies that they can use across a range of texts.

Aspect of comprehension	Examples of some strategies
Previewing/predicting	Picture walk Prediction grid Freeze frame 'what if?' moments
Activating and building prior knowledge	KWLT sheet True/false/don't know reflection quiz
Questioning (teacher to child, child to child and child to text)	Online character/topic forums Role play Sticky note flurry Questions to a character/author
Recall	Story boards Picture prompts Retell to a talk partner
Visualization and other sensory responses	Visual story maps Creating small world scenes/animations Sensory prompt sheet
Deducing, inferring and drawing conclusions	Compare and contrast activities Inference grid
Synthesizing	1+1=2 grid
Summarizing/determining importance	Main ideas wheel 50 words or less challenges Structured overviews
Empathizing	Relationship charts Character 'self portraits' 'I say, do, think and feel' charts
Personal responses including adopting a critical stance	Response book diaries Alternative ending activities 'What if the opposite were true?' debates Decision Alley

• Reading Fluency

Understanding the importance of building reading fluency and having explicit strategies to achieve this are relatively neglected aspects of learning to read. Fluency occurs as children begin to recognize more and more words automatically and are not slowed down by the need to decode words individually. This recognition includes words that have initially been worked out phonetically and high and medium frequency words that are not phonetically regular. Contextualized repetition of words throughout a text and across texts, and frequent opportunities to re-read texts, are important strategies for developing the fluency that comes with automatic word recognition. Word games and vocabulary building activities also play their part.

Further aspects of reading fluency are increasing the pace of reading from a slow word by word articulation, and the development of prosody – the rhythms and stresses used when reading (or talking) that help emphasize meaning. Some competent readers remain slow readers (in the sense of reading pace) or inexpressive readers. Initially, children might be expected to read fluently on texts which are familiar. This is one reason why opportunities to re-read texts are important. As their reading ability progresses this behaviour should begin to appear on unfamiliar texts.

At Y3/P4 the **Project X** books contain more complex language structures including both compound and complex sentences. More complex syntax offers opportunities to discuss the author's craft and the impact of particular language choices. Understanding decisions such as starting a sentence with 'Suddenly,' or the impact of embedding a phrase within a complex sentence helps children build expression and fluency into their reading and provides models for their writing.

The support materials for **Project X** draw on the latest research into developing fluency. Listening to books being read aloud is one of the most effective ways to support the development of fluency – as well as a love of books – in developing readers. As teachers read aloud they model expressive, fluent reading. Unfortunately, regularly reading aloud to the class may be something teachers struggle to find time for beyond the early years. It may also be absent at home. The **Project X** software offers audio visual versions of some of the character stories to provide models of fluent, expressive reading. The *Guided/Group Reading Notes* include ideas for developing pace and prosody through purposeful 'read aloud' activities, drama and role play. Children might also enjoy recording themselves reading the texts.

• Building vocabulary

Beyond a certain range of everyday vocabulary, most new vocabulary is encountered through reading. However, if any individual word is not understood – even if it can be decoded – it can cause problems with understanding of the sentence or passage or text. There is a vicious circle in which poor readers (often those with poor oral language as well) have a limited vocabulary and therefore encounter more words they don't understand in a text. This makes reading harder for these children and often puts them off reading when reading is the key to a wider vocabulary. Explicit work on enriching children's vocabulary – equipping them with a large bank of words they understand – is therefore vital to both comprehension and motivation.

Research recommends:

• teaching both specific words and word-learning strategies
• seeing and meeting new vocabulary in rich contexts provided by authentic texts
• using 'rich' vocabulary instruction i.e. going beyond just defining a word to get children actively engaged in using new words and thinking about word meanings
• fostering word consciousness by encouraging an awareness of and interest in words
• ensuring multiple exposures to words in multiple contexts.

The books and support materials for **Project X** incorporate all of these approaches and the cluster structure of the programme is ideal for reinforcing new vocabulary in a range of different contexts.

The interdependence of reading and writing

Reading and writing are mutually supportive skills – which is why those children who don't understand what it is to be a reader usually struggle to become writers. By helping to engage children in reading, **Project X** also aims to support and inspire children's writing.

Throughout the *Guided/Group Reading Notes* there are many opportunities to examine the writer's craft and voice, explore the use of literary and informational language and the use of varied vocabulary and sentence structures. After each book there are several fun and contextualized activities designed to develop children's writing skills – with both short and long writing tasks suggested. There is always a clear purpose for the writing task, and talk, role play and drama activities are included as a means to stimulate ideas. Oral composition and rehearsal with a talk partner are also encouraged.

The **Project X** books offer models for children's own writing and the themes and character books in particular provide plenty of inspiration.

Character assets and 'clip art' to support children's writing about the **Project X** characters can be found on the accompanying software. The stories on the software can also be explored with a whole class or groups of children and the writer's craft examined through editing and annotation of the text.

Themes and cross-curricular learning

One way of supporting children's learning is to help them see how different aspects of their learning link together. This gives breadth and depth to learning and enables children to see the relevance of what they are learning to their own lives, to other aspects of school learning and learning beyond school. Research indicates that boys in particular favour approaches to learning that help them recognize its releveance to their lives and make links. A cross-curricular approach to learning can help them to do this.

Project X has been designed around a cluster structure in which five books are linked by a theme. The themes have been chosen to be interesting and child-friendly, often reflecting their interests beyond school rather than strictly 'curricula' based themes. Nevertheless, links to the other subjects within the National Curriculum can be made, as can links to wider skills such as thinking, creativity and problem solving.

The *Guided/Group Reading Notes* for each cluster highlight the cross-curricular opportunities offered by each theme, and there are further ideas for developing a thematic approach on pages 64–68 of this Handbook.

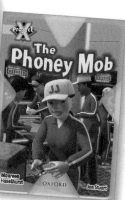

The importance of motivation

Learning to read can be a difficult task – as with all learning, some children will struggle more than others. But if children want to read, and see reading as a valuable and enjoyable activity, they are far more likely to be motivated to 'stick at it'. Research shows that being well motivated impacts on learning outcomes.

Project X aims to support motivation by offering high quality books that children will enjoy reading. The character books within the series (see pages 10–13) play a key part in this. Firstly, the development of a set of main characters provides role models children can identify with and will want to read about. Secondly, the character books include an intriguing 'soap' style plot that develops over several levels and is designed to motivate children to want to read on – to find out what happens. The non-fiction books also aim to intrigue and engage readers.

For some children, however, such motivational content is not enough on its own and external motivational strategies can help. Boys in particular respond well to praise and to motivational rewards. The **Project X** self assessment sheets (see pages 47–50) where children record their reading progress and **Project X** certificates (see pages 54-55) can all be used to boost motivation as well as record progress.

Creativity and thinking skills

There is worldwide recognition of the need for 21st century learners to develop the skills of 'learning to learn' rather than continuing to focus solely on subject knowledge. The follow-up activities suggested in the **Project X** *Guided/Group Reading Notes* for each book offer many opportunities to develop creative thinking and skills such as reasoning, evaluation and problem solving. The underpinning cross-curricular skill of communication is supported through the many suggestions for speaking and listening, drama and writing as well as suggestions for communicating through music and dance.

The overall structure of **Project X** – with the character story developing across clusters and throughout the levels – encourages creative thinking by offering possibilities for children to 'generate and extend ideas, suggest hypotheses, apply imagination, and look for alternative innovative outcomes'. (QCA definition of creative thinking)

The role of multimedia in children's lives and learning

Children are involved with IT and multimedia, multimodal texts well before they start school. Picture books, television, computer games and the Internet are so commonplace in modern homes that it is important to recognize and acknowledge these reading experiences and the specific literacy skills they require.

The 3D look and feel of the **Project X** character books is designed to bring the appeal of cartoons and computer games to reading – inspiring the 'Playstation Generation' to see books as a valid part of their learning and entertainment culture.

The **Project X** software provides a selection of the character stories as interactive electronic texts for use on a computer or interactive whiteboard. These texts include audio and animation that will really bring the stories to life for today's developing readers. Each story can be read through or listened to and then explored and annotated using the tools provided. To accompany each story is a collection of multimedia assets – video clips, audio, animation and images – to inspire talk and to help set the context for the story before reading. The software also contains a selection of 3D images from the character books for children to use in their own writing – either in print or on screen.

Creating a positive reading environment

An engaging and purposeful literacy environment is an important element of effective classrooms. It creates interest in reading and writing and offers many different opportunities for reading, writing, speaking and listening (including ICT based opportunities). It offers good models, learning prompts and resources to support learners in developing their literacy skills.

Such an environment includes an attractive book area with support materials and play/drama opportunities to encourage children to make links between their reading and wider learning. Role play areas are often abandoned as children move from the lower to upper primary year groups. Those primary classrooms that retain elements of role play practice, perhaps in the form of a themed area, report that these continue to stimulate creative responses, talk, drama and prompts into writing.

The cross-curricular charts for each cluster (see pages 65–68) give specific suggestions for the learning environment including a role play area that will encourage creative play and purposeful uses of literacy.

A wide range of texts

- Attractive, age-appropriate books, both fiction and non-fiction
- Collections of books linked to the theme/s being studied in class
- Other reading materials including comics, graphic novels, brochures, catalogues, magazines, manuals and so on
- Children's own published writing
- Audio and/or visual texts such as talking stories, films and videos
- Dictionaries, atlases and children's thesaurus

Role play or themed area

- Related to a theme, a book, or an environment
- Labels, signs and other appropriate environmental text
- Small world play figures, toys, construction equipment, puppets and other materials to encourage the enactment, extension and creation of stories and information
- Materials for writing

A good literacy environment includes:

Displays

- Posters, charts and so on related to particular books, characters and authors
- Learning prompts such as learning strategy posters, writing frameworks and so on
- Children's book reviews and other purposeful writing
- Labels, signs and notices for children to read in context

Vocabulary resources

- Word walls, word lists, word webs, word family charts
- Photographs and other images related to new vocabulary
- Word games - Scrabble, word snap. etc.
- Word of the Week and topic word displays

A comfy space

- Carpet, mats or cushions to make the reading area comfortable and inviting

The cluster structure of Project X

At all levels of **Project X**, the books are arranged in 'clusters' of five books that are linked by a theme. At Year 3/P4 there is one cluster (five books) at the transitional Lime Band and there are three clusters (fifteen books) at Brown Band.

Each cluster contains:

- 2 character stories
- I character non-fiction book
- I variety story (not including the core characters)
- I variety non-fiction book (not including the core characters)

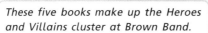

These five books make up the Heroes and Villains cluster at Brown Band.

All the books in a cluster are at the same reading level, although each book offers different aspects of support and challenge for the reader. The three clusters at Brown band provide ample consolidation as children become increasingly independent readers. Building confidence and fluency at a level helps readers become secure in their view of themselves as readers.

The benefits of this cluster approach are:

- the themes are designed to be interesting and motivating for young readers, particularly boys
- the mix of fiction and non-fiction books offers different ways in to a theme for different reading tastes – yet helps to encourage the reader's interest across a range of books
- the themes enable children to meet key new words many times in different contexts, thus building their range of and confidence with new vocabulary
- as the reader progresses through the books on a theme (in any sequence) their familiarity with the context and vocabulary grows – this increases their confidence as readers, improves their word recognition, comprehension and fluency skills, and ensures that every reader makes progress
- the themes offer rich contexts for talk, drama and writing
- the themes provide many meaningful links between literacy and the wider curriculum.

The cluster themes provided at Year 3/P4 are as follows:

Book Band	Oxford Reading Tree Stage	Project X Themes
II – Lime	Stage II	Masks and Disguises
12 – Brown	Stages 10-11	Strong Defences
		Heroes and Villains
		Fast and Furious

Using Project X for Guided reading

The **Project X** books have been written and levelled to help you deliver effective guided reading sessions, although they can also be used for independent reading.

Depending on how they are used, the books in each cluster cover roughly 6–8 weeks, based on average expectations of reading progression. Some children may progress more quickly through a level whilst others may need to spend more time at a level before moving on. It is important to undertake regular assessments of your guided reading groups to ensure that individual children are correctly supported and challenged.

Project X levels and progression in reading

Year Group					Book Band	National Curriculum Level
R/ P1	Y1/ P2	Y2/ P3	Y3/ P4	Y4/ P5		
■					Band 1 Pink	Working towards Level 1 (RA approx below 5 yrs)
■	▥				Band 2 Red	Working towards Level 1 (RA approx below 5 yrs)
■	▥				Band 3 Yellow	Working just within Level 1 (RA approx just 5 yrs)
░	■				Band 4 Blue	Working within Level 1 (RA approx 5 yrs +)
░	■	▥			Band 5 Green	Working within Level 1 (RA approx 5.5 yrs)
	■	▥			Band 6 Orange	Working towards Level 2 (RA approx 6 yrs)
	░	■			Band 7 Turquoise	Working towards Level 2 (RA approx 6.5 yrs)
		▥	■		Band 8 Purple	Working just within Level 2 (RA approx 7yrs)
		■			Band 9 Gold	Working within Level 2 (RA approx 7.5 yrs)
		■	▥	▥	Band 10 White	Working towards Level 3 (RA approx 8 yrs)
		░	■	▥	Band 11 Lime	Working towards and just within Level 3 (RA approx 8.5 yrs)
		░	■	▥	Band 12 Brown	Working within Level 3 (RA approx 9 -9.5 yrs)
			░	■	Band 13 Grey	Working towards Level 4 (RA approx 10 yrs +)

■ Expected Book Band range for majority of children in this year group

▥ Normal Band range for tracking back for less able readers in this year group

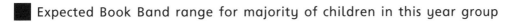

░ Normal Band range for tracking forward for more able readers in this year group

The books in each cluster can be used flexibly, depending on the needs and tastes of the guided reading group. You may want to encourage the group to select a book from the theme for each session. Or you may want to choose some books from the cluster for use in guided reading and use others for independent or paired reading.

With the longer texts, from Gold Band upwards, a book may be read over two or three guided reading sessions. Or only part of the book – a section or chapter – will be read in the guided reading session, preceded and/or followed by the rest of the book being read independently.

There are *Guided/Group Reading Notes* to support every book, with enough sessions to cover each book completely through guided reading if you wish to do so. There are also a wide range of ideas for follow-up work. How you manage this material, and how much of it you use, will depend on your overall needs and planning and the rate at which children's reading ability progresses.

Grouping children for guided reading

For guided reading sessions children are placed in groups of approximately six children of similar reading ability. Books are selected at the appropriate instructional level for each group – for guided reading, this means that children should be able to read the text with 90% accuracy. The Reading Behaviour checklist (see page 25) and/or the Running Record assessment sheets (see pages 59–60) can be used to help you establish and regularly assess the appropriate guided reading level for an individual child or group.

Once the correct instructional level is established most children will then progress through the **Project X** books, which have been carefully levelled to Book Bands to ensure a gradual increase in reading challenge. The books for each level contain many familiar words likely to be recognized automatically, plus an appropriate degree of challenge around which the guided teaching and learning will focus.

The *Guided/Group Reading Notes* provide support for the following teaching sequence for every book in a cluster:

- before reading
- during reading
- after reading
- follow-up work – including talk, drama, writing, ICT and cross-curricular activities.

For each book, there are clear learning objectives, targets and prompts for ongoing assessment linked to the QCA Reading Assessment focuses – an overview of the assessment focuses is given on pages 43–46 of this Handbook.

Independent reading

Children should be offered plenty of opportunities for wider independent reading of texts at a variety of levels. Re-reading familiar or favourite texts, even those considered 'easy', as well as sometimes tackling 'hard' but highly engaging texts, are necessary experiences for building confidence, fluency and a love of reading.

The **Project X** books are ideal for independent reading. But you will also want to make available a range of books from other programmes, favourite texts, picture books, information books, comic books, magazines, etc. for children to select from. Opportunities for children to make their own choice of books for independent reading is important in allowing them to develop the personal preferences essential to reading engagement.

Reading Behaviours Checklist

This checklist – supported by your own knowledge of each child – can be used at any time to assess children's reading behaviours in order to determine or review their guided reading level. Not all children in Year 3/P4 will be reading at Lime or Brown band, so behaviours are given to enable you to track back to earlier bands if required.

A child that is mostly **low** in the behaviours at a given band needs to be reading at a lower band.
A child that is mostly **secure** in the behaviours at a given band is at the right reading level.
A child that is mostly **high** in the behaviours at a given band needs to be reading at a higher band.

Name of child: Date:					
Book Band	**NC Level**	**Reading Behaviours**	**Low**	**Secure**	**High**
Purple/ Gold	Within Level 2	Can decode most new or unfamiliar words automatically			
		Can predict content of a variety of texts with increased independence			
		Can read silently or quietly with pace, using punctuation to keep track of longer passages			
		Begins to be aware of simple literary effects used by writers			
White/ Lime	Towards Level 3	Can read silently most of the time			
		Can automatically relate unknown words to known words			
		Can sustain interest in a longer text and return to it confidently after a break			
		Can search for and find information in a text			
		Shows increased awareness of wide range of vocabulary and precise meanings			
		Can give and discuss opinions about a text			
Brown	Within Level 3	Can sustain silent reading to include longer, more complex texts			
		Can read aloud with intonation and expression – particularly dialogue			
		Can recognize an increasing range of words automatically			
		Can identify ideas and themes within a text, making clear references			
		Can search for, find and evaluate information in a text			
		Can respond to and evaluate a text by making explicit references to the text			

Progression and planning

Primary Framework objectives chart

The chart below shows the key objectives from the **Primary Framework** that are covered in **Project X** at Year 3. Further objectives are covered in the many follow-up activities suggested in the *Guided/Group Reading Notes*.

The following Year 3 framework objective will be supported in every guided reading session and is therefore a continuous focus for attention and assessment.

- Use syntax and context to build their store of vocabulary when reading for meaning **7.4**

The following framework objectives from Year 2 (Strand 5, Word recognition) will continue to be consolidated in guided reading sessions in Year 3. Teachers will be aware of these objectives in their ongoing assessment but will only specifically assess against these objectives for children who are not making the expected rate of progress:

- Read independently and with increasing fluency longer and less familiar texts **5.1**
- Know how to tackle unfamiliar words that are not completely decodable **5.3**
- Read and spell less common alternative graphemes including trigraphs **5.4**
- Read high and medium frequency words independently and automatically **5.5**

Book band and theme	Title	Strands 1–4: Speaking, Listening, Group Interaction and Drama Objectives	Strands 5–8: Reading Objectives
Lime: Masks and Disguises	The Phoney Mob	• Use some drama strategies to explore stories or issues **4.2**	• Empathize with characters and debate moral dilemmas portrayed in texts **8.2** • Infer character's feelings in fiction **7.2**
	Stage Fright	• Use some drama strategies to explore stories or issues **4.2**	• Infer character's feelings in fiction **7.2**
	Masks in Film and Theatre	• Present information, ensuring that items are clearly sequenced, relevant details are included and accounts are ended effectively **1.2**	• Identify and make notes of the main points of sections of text **7.1** • Identify how different texts are organized **7.3** • Explore how different texts appeal to different readers using varied sentence structures and descriptive language **7.5**
	Sharks on the Loose!	• Sustain conversation, explain or give reasons for their views or choices **1.3**	• Empathize with characters and debate moral dilemmas portrayed in texts **8.2** • Recognize a range of prefixes and suffixes, understanding how they modify meaning and spelling, and how they assist in decoding long complex words **6.2**
	Safe Behind a Mask	• Sustain conversation, explain or give reasons for their views or choices **1.3**	• Identify how different texts are organized **7.3**

Book band and theme	Title	Strands 1–4: Speaking, Listening, Group Interaction and Drama Objectives	Strands 5–8: Reading Objectives
Brown: Fast and Furious	The Chase	● Explain process or present information, ensuring that items are clearly sequenced, relevant details are included and accounts are ended effectively 1.2	● Explore how different texts appeal to readers using varied sentence structures and descriptive language 7.5
	The Fun Run	● Develop and use specific vocabulary in different contexts 1.4	● Identify features that writers use to provoke reader's reactions 8.3
	Downhill Racers	● Explain process or present information, ensuring that items are clearly sequenced, relevant details are included and accounts are ended effectively 1.2	● Identify and make notes of the main points of sections of text 7.1 ● Select and use a range of technical and descriptive vocabulary 9.4
	The Super Skateplank	● Develop and use specific vocabulary in different contexts 1.4	● Infer character's feelings in fiction 7.2
	Top Speed	● Sustain conversation, explain or give reasons for their views or choices 1.3	● Identify how different texts are organized, including reference texts, magazines and leaflets on paper and on screen 7.3 ● Identify and make notes of the main points of sections of text 7.1
Brown: Heroes and Villains	Air Scare	● Explain process or present information, ensuring that items are clearly sequenced, relevant details are included and accounts are ended effectively 1.2	● Infer character's feelings in fiction 7.2 ● Empathize with characters and debate moral dilemmas portrayed in texts 8.2
	Heroine in Hiding	● Sustain conversation, explain or give reasons for their views or choices 1.3	● Infer character's feelings in fiction 7.2
	Dr X's Top 10 Villains	● Sustain conversation, explain or give reasons for their views or choices 1.3	● Identify how different texts are organized ● Share and compare reasons for reading preferences extending the range of books read 8.1
	Jake Jones v Vlad the Bad	● Develop and use specific vocabulary in different contexts 1.4	● Explore how different texts appeal to readers using varied sentence structures and descriptive language 7.5
	Heroes or Villains?	● Follow up others' points and show whether they agree or disagree in whole class discussion 2.1	● Empathize with characters and debate moral dilemmas portrayed in texts 8.2 ● Identify features that writers use to provoke readers' reactions 8.3

Book Band and theme	Title	Strands 1–4: Speaking, Listening, Group Interaction and Drama Objectives	Strands 5–8: Reading Objectives
Brown: Strong Defences	The X-bots are Coming	● Use some drama strategies to explore stories or issues **4.2**	● Empathize with characters **8.2** ● Identify features writers use to provoke readers' reactions **8.3**
	Attack of the X bots!	● Explain processes or present information ensuring that items are clearly sequenced, relevant details are included and accounts are ended effectively **1.2**	● Infer character's feelings in fiction **7.2** ● Empathize with characters **8.2** ● Identify features that writers use to provoke readers' reactions **8.3**
	Under Attack!	● Develop and use specific vocabulary in different contexts **1.4** ● Follow up others' points and show whether they agree or disagree **2.1**	● Identify and make notes of the main points of sections of texts **7.1**
	Lone Wolf	● Use the language of possibility to investigate and reflect on feelings, behaviour or relationships **3.3**	● Infer character's feelings **7.2** ● Empathize with characters **8.2** ● Explore how different texts appeal to readers using varied sentence structures and descriptive language **7.5**
	Strong Defences	● Identify the presentational features used to communicate the main points in a broadcast **2.3**	● Identify how different texts are organized **7.3** ● Share and compare reasons for reading preferences **8.1**

Project X and Curriculum for Excellence

Project X has been carefully developed to reflect and support the purposes and principles of the new Scottish curriculum: *Curriculum for Excellence.*

The charts on pages 31-35 show how the English curriculum objectives used in the Year 3/Primary 4 *Guided/Group Reading Notes* correlate to the **Curriculum for Excellence Draft Experiences and Outcomes for Literacy and English**. As the experiences and outcomes are finalised, we will update this correlation.
(See www.OxfordPrimary.co.uk/projectx)

Enjoyment and choice

Recent research by both PISA and the Scottish Survey of Assessment has demonstrated that boys in Scotland are falling behind girls in reading. It also showed that boys are less likely to regard themselves as readers and are less motivated to read. The **Project X** books offer an exciting and motivating choice of content for all your pupils, whilst placing particular emphasis on the needs and tastes of boy readers.

Literacy across the curriculum

The thematic 'cluster' structure of **Project X** supports the application of literacy across the curriculum and provides opportunities for children to learn and apply topic-specific vocabulary. Through its inclusion of cross-curricular activities and links to other subject areas, **Project X** encourages children to develop and apply literacy skills across other curriculum subjects and to become successful learners. The *Guided/Group Reading Notes* provide a range of follow-up activities, many of which are active and hands-on, to support the practical application of literacy skills in a range of contexts. Further ideas for taking this approach to learning are given on pages 64–68 of this Handbook.

A range of text types and ICT opportunities

Project X includes a range of fiction and non-fiction text types and a variety of author styles to ensure that children are exposed to different kinds of text. In addition, the **Project X** *Interactive Stories* software includes interactive electronic versions of some of the core **Project X** stories, giving you the opportunity to embed ICT into your literacy lessons. The *Guided/Group Reading Notes* also provide ICT activities, such as writing an email or using digital photographs to form the basis of a print or ICT text.

Listening and talking

The **Project X** *Guided/Group Reading Notes* place a strong emphasis on the importance of listening and talking both as a precursor to successful reading, comprehension and writing and as a means of ensuring that children become confident individuals and effective contributors. Children are encouraged to talk before, during and after reading, to express preferences and to give and justify their opinions of a book. In addition, there are opportunities for collaborative partner and group work, for giving presentations and for drama activities.

Critical literacy skills

The latest *Curriculum for Excellence* guidance emphasises the importance of critical literacy. The **Project X** *Guided/Group Reading Notes* provide explicit opportunities for the development of comprehension strategies before, during and after reading; encouraging children to read critically and become successful learners.

Assessment is For Learning AiFL / Personalisation

Project X provides extensive assessment support. The *Guided/Group Reading Notes* suggest assessment focuses for reading and listening and talking for every **Project X** book. In addition, there are opportunities to practise self and peer assessment and support for such is provided on page 42 and pages 48-50 of this Handbook. It should be noted that the wording of the target and assessment focuses can and should be adapted to suit individual learning needs.

Guided/Group Reading

The **Project X** *Guided/Group Reading Notes* provide a model for teachers of how to run a successful guided/group reading session. In line with the latest *Curriculum for Excellence* guidance, **Project X** provides explicit opportunities for the development of reading strategies before, during and after reading. Also included in the *Guided/Group Reading Notes* are a range of follow-up activities to support the link from reading into writing, talking and into other curriculum areas.

Book Band and theme	Title		Objectives used in the Guided/Group Reading Notes	Curriculum for Excellence draft guidelines
Lime: Masks and Disguises	The Phoney Mob	Listening and talking objectives	● Use some drama strategies to explore stories or issues	● When listening and talking with others, for different purposes, I can exchange information, experiences, explanations, ideas and opinions LIT 109J
		Reading objectives	● Empathize with characters and debate moral dilemmas portrayed in texts ● Infer characters' feelings in fiction	● I can share my thoughts about structure, characters and/or setting ENG 119V
	Stage Fright	Listening and talking objectives	● Use some drama strategies to explore stories or issues	● When listening and talking with others, for different purposes, I can exchange information, experiences, explanations, ideas and opinions LIT 109J
		Reading objectives	● Infer character's feelings in fiction	● I can share my thoughts about structure, characters and/or setting ENG 119V
	Masks in Film and Theatre	Listening and talking objectives	● Present information, ensuring that items are clearly sequenced, relevant details are included and accounts are ended effectively	● I can select ideas and relevant information, organize these in a logical sequence and use words which will be interesting and/or useful for others LIT 106F
		Reading objectives	● Identify and make notes of the main points of sections of text ● Identify how different texts are organized ● Explore how different texts appeal to different readers using varied sentence structures and descriptive language	● To show my understanding across different areas of learning, I can identify and consider the purpose and main ideas of my text LIT 116S ● Using what I know about the features of different texts, I can find, select sort and use information for a specific purpose LIT 114Q ● I can comment on the effective choice of words and other features ENG 119V
	Sharks on the Loose!	Listening and talking objectives	● Sustain conversation, explain or give reasons for their views or choices	● When listening and talking with others, for different purposes, I can exchange information, experiences, explanations, ideas and opinions LIT 109J
		Reading objectives	● Empathize with characters and debate moral dilemmas portrayed in texts ● Recognize a range of prefixes and suffixes, understanding how they modify meaning and spelling, and how they assist in decoding long complex words	● I can share my thoughts about structure, characters and/or setting ENG 119V ● I can use my knowledge of sight vocabulary, phonics, context clues, punctuation and grammar to read with understanding and expression LIT 112N

Book Band and theme	Title		Objectives used in the Guided/Group Reading Notes	Curriculum for Excellence draft guidelines
Lime: Masks and Disguises	Safe Behind a Mask	Listening and talking objectives	● Sustain conversation, explain or give reasons for their views or choices	● When listening and talking with others, for different purposes, I can exchange information, experiences, explanations, ideas and opinions **LIT 109J**
		Reading objectives	● Identify how different texts are organized	● Using what I know about the features of different texts, I can find, select sort and use information for a specific purpose **LIT 114Q**
Brown: Fast and Furious	The Chase	Listening and talking objectives	● Explain process or present information, ensuring that items are clearly sequenced, relevant details are included and accounts are ended effectively	● I can select ideas and relevant information, organize these in a logical sequence and use words which will be interesting and/or useful for others **LIT 106F**
		Reading objectives	● Explore how different texts appeal to readers using varied sentence structures and descriptive language	● I can comment on the effective choice of words and other features **ENG 119V**
	The Fun Run	Listening and talking objectives	● Develop and use specific vocabulary in different contexts	● I can select ideas and relevant information, organize these in a logical sequence and use words which will be interesting and/or useful for others **LIT 106F**
		Reading objectives	● Identify features that writers use to provoke readers' reactions	● I can recognize the writer's message and relate it to my own experiences **ENG 119V** ● I can comment on the effective choice of words and other features **ENG 119V**
	Downhill Racers	Listening and talking objectives	● Explain process or present information, ensuring that items are clearly sequenced, relevant details are included and accounts are ended effectively	● I can select ideas and relevant information, organize these in a logical sequence and use words which will be interesting and/or useful for others **LIT 106F**
		Reading objectives	● Identify and make notes of the main points of sections of text ● Select and use a range of technical and descriptive vocabulary	● To show my understanding across different areas of learning, I can identify and consider the purpose and main ideas of my text **LIT 116S** ● Using what I know about the features of different types of texts, I can find, select, sort and use information for a specific purpose **LIT 114Q**
	The Super Skateplank	Listening and talking objectives	● Develop and use specific vocabulary in different contexts	● I can select ideas and relevant information, organize these in a logical sequence and use words which will be interesting and/or useful for others **LIT 106F**
		Reading objectives	● Infer character's feelings in fiction	● I can share my thoughts about structure, characters and/or setting **ENG 119V**

Book Band and theme	Title		Objectives used in the Guided/Group Reading Notes	Curriculum for Excellence draft guidelines
Brown: Fast and Furious	Top Speed	Listening and talking objectives	● Sustain conversation, explain or give reasons for their views or choices	● When listening and talking with others, for different purposes, I can exchange information, experiences, explanations, ideas and opinions **LIT 109J**
		Reading objectives	● Identify how different texts are organized, including reference texts, magazines and leaflets on paper and on screen ● Identify and make notes of the main points of sections of text	● Using what I know about the features of different texts, I can find, select sort and use information for a specific purpose **LIT 114Q** ● I am learning to make notes under given headings and use these to understand information, explore ideas and problems and create new texts **LIT 115R** ● To show my understanding across different areas of learning, I can identify and consider the purpose and main ideas of my text **LIT 116S**
Brown: Heroes and Villains	Air Scare	Listening and talking objectives	● Explain process or present information, ensuring that items are clearly sequenced, relevant details are included and accounts are ended effectively	● I can select ideas and relevant information, organize these in a logical sequence and use words which will be interesting and/or useful for others **LIT 106F**
		Reading objectives	● Infer characters' feelings in fiction ● Empathize with characters and debate moral dilemmas portrayed in texts	● I can share my thoughts about structure, characters and/or setting **ENG 119V**
	Heroine in Hiding	Listening and talking objectives	● Sustain conversation, explain or give reasons for their views or choices	● When listening and talking with others, for different purposes, I can exchange information, experiences, explanations, ideas and opinions **LIT 109J**
		Reading objectives	● Infer characters' feelings in fiction	● I can share my thoughts about structure, characters and/or setting **ENG 119V**
	Dr X's Top 10 Villains	Listening and talking objectives	● Sustain conversation, explain or give reasons for their views or choices	● When listening and talking with others, for different purposes, I can exchange information, experiences, explanations, ideas and opinions **LIT 109J**
		Reading objectives	● Identify how different texts are organized ● Share and compare reasons for reading preferences extending the range of books read	● Using what I know about the features of different texts, I can find, select sort and use information for a specific purpose **LIT 114Q** ● I regularly select and read, listen to or watch texts which I enjoy and find interesting, and I can explain why I prefer certain texts and authors **ENG 11M**

Book Band and theme	Title		Objectives used in the Guided/Group Reading Notes	Curriculum for Excellence draft guidelines
Brown: Heroes and Villains	Jake Jones v Vlad the Bad	Listening and talking objectives	● Develop and use specific vocabulary in different contexts	● I can select ideas and relevant information, organize these in a logical sequence and use words which will be interesting and/or useful for others **LIT 106F**
		Reading objectives	● Explore how different texts appeal to readers using varied sentence structures and descriptive language	● I can comment on the effective choice of words and other features **ENG 119V**
	Heroes or Villains?	Listening and talking objectives	● Follow up others' points and show whether they agree or disagree in whole class discussion	● When listening and talking with others, for different purposes, I can exchange information, experiences, explanations, ideas and opinions **LIT 109J**
		Reading objectives	● Empathize with characters and debate moral dilemmas portrayed in texts ● Identify features that writers use to provoke readers' reactions	● I can share my thoughts about structure, characters and/or setting **ENG 119V** ● I can recognize the writer's message and relate it to my own experiences **ENG 119V** ● I can comment on the effective choice of words and other features **ENG 119V**
Brown: Strong Defences	The X-bots are Coming	Listening and talking objectives	● Use some drama strategies to explore stories or issues	● When listening and talking with others, for different purposes, I can exchange information, experiences, explanations, ideas and opinions **LIT 109J**
		Reading objectives	● Empathize with characters ● Identify features writers use to provoke readers' reactions	● I can share my thoughts about structure, characters and/or setting **ENG 119V** ● I can recognize the writer's message and relate it to my own experiences **ENG 119V** ● I can comment on the effective choice of words and other features **ENG 119V**
	Attack of the X-bots!	Listening and talking objectives	● Explain processes or present information ensuring that items are clearly sequenced, relevant details are included and accounts are ended effectively	● I can select ideas and relevant information, organize these in a logical sequence and use words which will be interesting and/or useful for others **LIT 106F**
		Reading objectives	● Infer character's feelings in fiction ● Empathize with characters ● Identify features that writers use to provoke readers' reactions	● I can share my thoughts about structure, characters and/or setting **ENG 119V** ● I can recognize the writer's message and relate it to my own experiences **ENG 119V** ● I can comment on the effective choice of words and other features **ENG 119V**

Book Band and theme	Title		Objectives used in the Guided/Group Reading Notes	Curriculum for Excellence draft guidelines
Brown: Strong Defences	Under Attack!	Listening and talking objectives	• Develop and use specific vocabulary in different contexts • Follow up others' points and show whether they agree or disagree	• I can select ideas and relevant information, organize these in a logical sequence and use words which will be interesting and/or useful for others **LIT 106F** • When listening and talking with others, for different purposes, I can exchange information, experiences, explanations, ideas and opinions **LIT 109J**
		Reading objectives	• Identify and make notes of the main points of sections of texts	• I am learning to make notes under given headings and use these to understand information, explore ideas and problems and create new texts **LIT 115R** • To show my understanding across different areas of learning, I can identify and consider the purpose and main ideas of my text **LIT 116S**
	Lone Wolf	Listening and talking objectives	• Use the language of possibility to investigate and reflect on feelings, behaviour or relationships	• When listening and talking with others, for different purposes, I can exchange information, experiences, explanations, ideas and opinions **LIT 109J**
		Reading objectives	• Infer character's feelings • Empathize with characters • Explore how different texts appeal to readers using varied sentence structures and descriptive language	• I can share my thoughts about structure, characters and/or setting **ENG 119V** • I can comment on the effective choice of words and other features **ENG 119V**
	Strong Defences	Listening and talking objectives	• Identify the presentational features used to communicate the main points in a broadcast	• As I listen or watch, I can identify and discuss the purpose, key words and main ideas of the text **LIT 104D**
		Reading objectives	• Identify how different texts are organized • Share and compare reasons for reading preferences	• Using what I know about the features of different texts, I can find, select sort and use information for a specific purpose **LIT 114Q** • I regularly select and read, listen to or watch texts which I enjoy and find interesting, and I can explain why I prefer certain texts and authors **ENG 11M**

Project X and the National Curriculum in Wales

Project X has been developed to support the desired English outcomes of the new *National Curriculum for Wales* (2008).

The chart opposite shows how the **Project X** clusters at Year 3 Lime/Brown bands correlates to the skills and outcomes for Oracy and Reading required by the **Key Stage 2 Programme of Study.**

Talking, communicating and listening

The *National Curriculum for Wales* emphasises the importance of talk and other forms of communication in developing children's literacy and wider social skills. By Key Stage 2, learners are becoming confident, coherent and engaging speakers and active and responsive listeners.

The **Project X** books have been designed to stimulate talk, drama and role play and there is support within the books for exploring characters and settings, raising and responding to questions, and expressing opinions. The *Guided/Group Reading Notes* provide a wealth of opportunities for using talk both as a precursor to successful reading, comprehension and writing, and as a means to ensure that children become confident individuals and effective contributors.

Skills across the curriculum

The new *National Curriculum for Wales* promotes a holistic view of children's learning and encourages the development of skills in a range of contexts. Learners should be given opportunities to build on the skills acquired in the Foundation Phase and continue to acquire, develop, practise, apply and refine these skills as they progress through Key Stage 2.

The thematic 'cluster' structure of **Project X** provides opportunities for children to develop and practise a range of literacy skills – together with broader skills such as thinking and communication – within a familiar context, and then to apply these skills across the curriculum. The *Guided/Group Reading Notes* provide a range of 'after reading' follow-up activities, many of which are active and hands on, to support the application of skills in a range of contexts.

A wide range of print and media experiences

Project X offers children a wide choice of exciting fiction and non-fiction books that are designed to engage all readers, particularly the boys. Children are exposed to different ways of presenting information, are encouraged to 'read the pictures', and supported in making links between different books in the series. The use of digital artwork for the character stories brings the world of modern media to reading books, making them relevant to children whose experiences outside school – even from a very young age – often involve very sophisticated media.

The **Project X** *Interactive Stories* software presents a collection of stories supported by audio and animation, plus links to video clips, images and audio files.

Writing

Throughout **Project X** the importance of linking reading to writing is emphasised. At Key Stage 2, children acquire a broader range of skills and become competent writers across a range of forms and purposes. The **Project X** books at Lime and Brown bands aim to provide both inspiration for and models of writing to support children's writing development. The *Guided/Group Reading Notes* provide a range of follow up writing activities from which you can choose the most appropriate for your pupils.

Book Band and Cluster Themes	National Curriculum Level	English Skills	Attainment targets
Lime Band: **Masks and Disguises** **Brown Band:** **Fast and Furious** **Heroes and Villains** **Strong Defences**	Working towards or within Level 3 Working within Level 3	**Oracy:** • Listen and view attentively, responding to a wider range of communication • Identify key points and follow up ideas through question and comment, developing response to others in order to learn through talk • Communicate clearly and confidently, expressing opinions, adapting talk to audience and purpose • Use a range of sentence structures and vocabulary with precision, including terminology that allows them to discuss their work • Evaluate their own and others' talk and drama activities; consider how speakers adapt their vocabulary, tone and pace to a range of situations **Reading:** • Develop phonic, graphic and grammatical knowledge, word recognition and contextual understanding • Read with fluency, accuracy, understanding and enjoyment • Read in different ways for different purposes • Recognize and understand the characteristics of different genres in terms of language, structure and presentation • Consider and respond to what they read, selecting evidence from the text to support their views • Use a range of appropriate information retrieval strategies • Retrieve and collate information and ideas from a range of sources • Use knowledge from reading to develop an understanding of vocabulary, grammar and punctuation and how these clarify meaning • Consider how texts change when they are adapted for different media and audiences	**Oracy:** **Level 3** • Talk and listen confidently in different contexts • Explore and communicate ideas • Show an understanding of the main points of a discussion • Show that they have listened carefully • Adapt what they say to the needs of the listener • Express opinions simply and clearly **Reading:** **Level 3** • Read a range of texts fluently and accurately • Use appropriate strategies to read independently and establish meaning • Show understanding of the main points of a text • Express opinions and preferences • Locate books and find information

Project X and the Northern Ireland Primary Curriculum

Project X is fully in line with the aims and objectives of the **Revised Primary Curriculum for Northern Ireland**.

Cross-curricular skills and a thematic approach

The thematic 'cluster' structure of **Project X** supports the application of literacy across the curriculum and provides opportunities for children to learn and apply a range of skills. The structure also helps children to become successful learners – it builds confidence through the familiarity of a theme, supports progression and is highly motivating. The *Guided/Group Reading Notes* provide a range of follow-up activities to support the application of literacy skills in a range of contexts.

Further ideas for taking a thematic approach to learning are given on pages 64-68 of this Handbook.

Engaging pupils in active learning

Project X aims to engage and involve children as readers and as learners. The books themselves are full of action and adventure which is particularly appealing to boys, whilst the *Guided/Group Reading Notes* encourage active learning both during and as a follow-up to group reading sessions. Ideas for drama, talk and things to 'make and do' in response to books are given throughout the programme.

Talking and listening

The importance of talk and other forms of communication in developing children's literacy and wider social skills is widely recognized. The **Project X** books have been designed to stimulate talk and role play and there is support within the books for exploring characters, retelling stories, raising and responding to questions, and expressing opinions. The *Guided/Group Reading Notes* provide a wealth of opportunities for using talk both as a precursor to successful reading, comprehension and writing, and as a means of ensuring that children become confident individuals and effective contributors.

Reading a wide range of texts

Project X offers children a wide choice of exciting fiction and non-fiction books that are designed to engage all readers, particularly the boys. Children are exposed to different ways of presenting information, are encouraged to 'read the pictures', and supported in making links between different books in the series. The use of digital artwork for the character stories brings the world of modern media to reading books, making them relevant to children whose experiences outside school – even from a very young age – often involve very sophisticated media.

The **Project X** *Interactive Stories* software presents a collection of stories supported by audio and animation, plus links to video clips, images and audio files.

Thinking, problem solving and decision making

The character stories within **Project X** present readers with a range of scenarios in which our core characters are faced with problems, challenges and decisions to make. By following the adventures of Max, Cat, Ant and Tiger readers can learn to empathise with situations and explore their own problem solving skills.

Working with others

Throughout **Project X** there is an emphasis on collaborative learning. The *Guided/ Group Reading Notes* provide lots of opportunities for pair and group work linked to talk, reading, drama and writing. Within this Handbook there are also ideas for using peer assessment – see page 42.

Positive attitudes to learning

Project X aims to help all children, particularly the boys, adopt a positive attitude to learning. The highly original and engaging books and software are designed to make all children want to read and to be enthusiastic about the learning process. **Project X** also supports and encourages teachers to have high expectations of all their pupils – something shown to have a powerful impact on young learners.

Statutory Requirements for Language and Literacy at Key Stage 1

Project X can help you deliver on the following statutory requirements for Talking and Listening and Reading. It also provides a range of follow-up activities to support children's writing.

Talking and listening

- Participate in talking and listening in every area of learning
- Listen to, respond to and explore stories
- Listen to, interpret and retell with some supporting detail, a range of texts
- Tell stories based on personal experience and imagination
- Take turns at talking and listening in group and pair activities
- Take part in a range of drama activities to support learning across the curriculum
- Express thoughts, feelings and opinions
- Present ideas and information with some structure and sequence
- Think about what they say and how they say it
- Speak audibly and clearly using appropriate speech and voice
- Devise and ask questions to find information
- Read aloud from a variety of sources, inflecting appropriately to emphasize meaning
- Recognize and talk abut the features of spoken language

Reading

- Participate in modelled, shared, paired and guided reading experiences
- Read with some independence for enjoyment and information
- Read, explore, understand and make use of a range of texts
- Retell, re-read and act out a range of texts through drama
- Begin to locate, select and use texts for specific purposes
- Research and manage information relevant to specific purposes
- Use a range of comprehension skills to interpret and discuss texts
- Explore and begin to understand how texts are structured in a range of genres
- Express opinions and give reasons – beginning to use evidence from the text
- Build up a sight vocabulary
- Use a range of strategies to identify unfamiliar words
- Talk about ways in which language is written down, identifying phrases, words, patterns or letters and other features of written language
- Recognize how words are constructed and spelt

Assessing Pupils' Progress

Approaches to assessment

Teachers constantly assess pupils by observing what they can do, what they struggle with and what they can't do. Evidence of achievement is collected in a variety of ways and then evaluated. Finally teachers (and sometimes children) form a judgement on the basis of that evidence. Such assessment processes are an everyday part of classroom practice and should involve both teachers and learners in reflection, dialogue and decision-making.

Sometimes judgements are used for summative assessment purposes – to 'sum up' what a child can do at a given point in time. Others are used for formative assessment purposes – for learners and their teachers to decide where the learners are in their learning, where they need to go and how best to get there. These two purposes of assessment are often described as assessment *of* learning and assessment *for* learning.

Assessment for learning opportunities are fully integrated into the guided/group reading sessions in **Project X**. Clearly identified 'child speak' targets (directly related to the teaching objectives) are given to ensure that both the learner and the teacher understand what is to be learnt. Assessing against the target provides opportunities for both learner and teacher to comment and reflect on progress towards the learning goal/s. If they know their learning goal and how it will be assessed children can be involved in self assessment and peer assessment. Teachers should give feedback against the targets; discuss what the learner has achieved in relation to the target and what they should do next to progress in their learning. Giving positive feedback against targets helps focus on the work rather than the person which is more constructive for both learning and motivation. Assessment for learning information feeds back into the planning process (what does the child need to do next?).

Using Assessment Focuses

The assessment for learning opportunities within the guided/group reading sessions are linked to the reading assessment focuses (AFs) that inform the National Curriculum levels for English. This means the evidence gathered during these assessment opportunities can also feed into a structured approach to *periodically* assessing reading against national criteria. This approach is currently being promoted by the Primary National Strategy and QCA in *Assessing Pupil Progress* (APP).

An assessment approach based on AFs enables you to build a detailed profile of what the child can do in relation to the AFs. From this you can assign an evidence-based National Curriculum level for each child based on an informed holistic judgement rather than relying solely on tests and tasks. You can track pupils' progress through the levels and use diagnostic information about their strengths and weaknesses to inform planning. Many Year 3 teachers are already skilled in judging their children's work against AFs and assign a National Curriculum level based on both the summative assessment evidence of the national tests and periodic assessments made within a curriculum context. **Project X** helps you build this into your guided/group reading sessions.

The AF chart on page 41 shows the detailed elements of each reading assessment focus so that you can match the qualities you have noted in a child's reading against these criteria. The chart can be used to inform and record your judgements against specific assessment focuses and extrapolate these to accurately assess a pupil's National Curriculum level.

	AF1 – use a range of strategies, including accurate decoding of text, to read for meaning	AF2 – understand, describe, select or retrieve information, events or ideas from texts and use quotation and reference to text.	AF3 – deduce, infer or interpret information, events or ideas from text	AF4 – identify and comment on the structure and organisation of texts, including grammatical and presentational features at text level	AF5 – explain and comment on writer's use of language, including grammatical and literary features at word and sentence level	AF6 – identify and comment on writers' purposes and viewpoints, and the overall effect of the text on the reader	AF7 – relate texts to their social, cultural and historical traditions
Level 3	**In most reading** • range of strategies used most effectively to read with fluency, understanding and expression	**In most reading** • simple, most obvious points identified though there may also be some misunderstanding, e.g. *about information from different places in the text* • some comments include quotations from or references to text, but not always relevant, e.g. *often retelling or paraphrasing sections of that text rather than using it to support comment*	**In most reading** • straightforward inference based on a single point of reference in the text, e.g. *'he was upset because it says "he was crying"'*; • responses to text show meaning established at a literal level e.g. *"walking good" means "walking carefully"* or based on personal speculation e.g. *a response based on what they personally would be feeling rather than feelings of character in the text*	**In most reading** • a few basis features of organisation at text level identified, with little or no linked comment, e.g. *'it tells about all the different things you can do at the zoo'*	**In most reading** • a few basis features of writer's use of language identified, but with little or no comments, e.g. *'there are lots of adjectives' or #the uses speech marks to show there are lots of people there'*	**In most reading** • comments identify main purpose, e.g. *'the writer doesn't like violence'* • express personal response but with little awareness of writer's viewpoint or effect on reader, e.g. *'she was just horrible like my Nan is sometimes'*	**In most reading** • some simple connections between texts identified, e.g. similarities in plot, topic, or books by same author, about same characters • recognitions of some features of the context of texts, e.g. historical setting, social or cultural background
Level 2	**In some reading** • range of key words read on sight • unfamiliar words decoded using appropriate strategies, e.g. *blending sounds* • some fluency and expression, e.g. *taking account of speech marks, punctuation*	**In some reading** • some specific, straightforward information recalled, e.g. *names of characters, main ingredients* • generally clear idea of where to look for information, e.g. *about characters, topics*	**In some reading** • simple, plausible inference about events and information, using evidence from text, e.g. *how a character is feeling, what makes a plant grow* • comments based on textual clues, sometimes misunderstood	**In some reading** • some awareness of use of features of organisation, e.g. *beginning and ending of story, types of punctuation*	**In some reading** • some effective language choices noted, e.g. *"slimy" is a good word there'* • some familiar patterns of language identified, e.g. *once upon a time, first, next, last*	**In some reading** • some awareness that writers have viewpoints and purposes, e.g. *'it tells you how to do something', 'she thinks it's not fair'*	**In some reading** • general features of a few text types identified, e.g. information books, stories, print media • some awareness that books are set in different times and places
BL							
IE							

Key: BL – Below Level IE – Insufficient Evidence

Overall assessment (tick one box only)

Low 2	Secure 2	High 2	Low 3	Secure 3	High 3
☐	☐	☐	☐	☐	☐

Assessing and recording against targets

Turning objectives into clear, child-relevant targets and sharing these targets with the learner enables children to understand the focus for their learning. It also helps to engage children in reflecting on whether they have achieved their goals and made progress. This is particularly important to boys, who need to see a clear purpose for their learning and clear evidence of their own success.

Within the **Project X** *Guided/Group Reading Notes* are speaking and listening and reading targets related to the teaching objectives. On the following pages, you will find photocopiable assessment sheets for each cluster of books. These can be used for group or individual assessment against the targets. The assessment can be done during a guided/group reading session as you listen to individual children read and observe their participation in and understanding of the pre- and post-reading activities.

Self and peer assessment

Encouraging learners to self evaluate and to become involved in positive assessment of their peers is an important part of assessment for learning. It encourages learners to reflect on their targets and judge themselves against criteria relevant to the target. This helps them understand that assessment is not an arbitrary process. It also helps them become self aware and self critical. They develop an understanding that assessment can help them see how to improve by focusing on what they have done well and where/how they can get better.

On pages 47–50 you will find a series of photocopiable self assessment sheets so that children can record and track their own progress against their reading targets for each cluster in year 3. These sheets can also be used for peer-assessment. The self assessment sheets can be stuck in the front of children's literacy books or reading diaries and children encouraged to self assess against one or two of the reading targets each week. What to record on their self assessment sheet should result from a discussion with an adult or a reading partner, following a reading session.

Assessing and recording comprehension skills

The *Guided/Group Reading Notes* that accompany the **Project X** books identify the comprehension strategies that are being developed as readers undertake various activities before, during and after reading. The comprehension assessment chart (see page 51) can be used at regular intervals – for example, on completion of a cluster of books or every half term – to assess the comprehension skills of the guided reading group or of individual children. This chart will enable you to see at a glance those skills which are well established and those that require further support.

In future sessions, you can then select the appropriate activities from the many comprehension opportunities suggested in the *Guided/Group Reading Notes*, to support the skills needing further development.

The comprehension assessment chart also allows teachers to record whether learners are developing the metacognitive skills of identifying an appropriate strategy to use and assessing its effectiveness.

PROJECT X – Guided reading targets and assessment record
LIME BAND: MASKS AND DISGUISES

Book	Reading target We can ...	Name of child or group: HIGH	SECURE	LOW	Comments
The Phoney Mob **Date**	Use drama to help us understand how characters behave **AF3**				
	Talk about how characters feel and discuss why they might make particular decisions **AF3**				
	Draw conclusions about the characteristics of a person **AF3**				
Stage Fright **Date**	Use drama to help us understand how characters behave **AF3**				
	Draw conclusions about the characteristics of a person **AF3**				
	Collect new vocabulary from reading **AF2**				
Masks in Film and Theatre **Date**	Give the details of a chapter in the appropriate sequence **AF2**				
	Make notes to summarize the main points of a section **AF2**				
	Distinguish between different kinds of text in a book and say how they are organized **AF4**				
	Identify effective sentences and descriptive language in reading **AF5**				
Sharks on the Loose! **Date**	Comment on the writer's point of view **AF6**				
	Understand how the characters' feelings change during the story **AF3**				
	Use our knowledge of prefixes and suffixes to help decode words **AF1**				
Safe Behind a Mask **Date**	Attempt to answer each others' questions, giving reasons **AF2/3**				
	Talk about and evaluate the different ways that the text has been organized in the book **AF4**				
	Read words using different ways to help **AF1**				

PROJECT X – Guided reading targets and assessment record
BROWN BAND: FAST AND FURIOUS

Book	Reading target We can ...	Name of child or group:			
		HIGH	SECURE	LOW	Comments
The Chase Date	Explain the main events of the story in a clear sequence **AF2/4**				
	Collect new vocabulary from our reading **AF3/5**				
	Identify effective sentences and descriptive language in our reading **AF5**				
The Fun Run Date	Use exciting vocabulary to record a racing commentary **AF3/5**				
	Collect new vocabulary from our reading **AF2**				
	Find ways in which a writer makes the reader react to the story **AF6**				
Downhill Racers Date	Gather information from a text and present this to others **AF2/3**				
	Identify the main points in a text, and make notes of these **AF2/3**				
	Collect new vocabulary from our reading **AF2**				
The Super Skateplank Date	Use vocabulary to describe the different emotions and feelings of the characters **AF3/5**				
	Infer how characters are feeling about themselves and others **AF3**				
	Collect new vocabulary from our reading **AF2**				
Top Speed Date	Take part in a conversation and give reasons for why we think something **AF3**				
	Identify different features of a non-fiction text such as tables, facts, illustrated diagrams etc **AF4**				
	Summarize the main points of a text **AF2**				

PROJECT X – Guided reading targets and assessment record
BROWN BAND: HEROES AND VILLAINS

Book	Reading target	Name of child or group:			
	We can ...	HIGH	SECURE	LOW	Comments
Air Scare **Date**	Relate the events of the story and express events in a clear order **AF2**				
	Work out how characters might be feeling and give our reasons **AF2/3**				
	Identify the moral dilemma in a story and talk about how we would feel if we were in a similar situation **AF2/3**				
Heroine in Hiding **Date**	Take part in a discussion and respond to questions, giving reasons for our answers **AF3**				
	Work out how characters might be feeling and give our reasons **AF2/3**				
	Discuss the words the author has used **AF5**				
Dr X's Top 10 Villains **Date**	Talk about our views and give reasons for our choices **AF2**				
	Know some of the ways that reference texts organize their information **AF4**				
	Talk about the effect of different texts on the reader **AF6**				
Jake Jones v Vlad the Bad **Date**	Choose and use words to fit the context **AF2**				
	Make sense of and use words collected from our reading **AF1/2**				
	Identify effective sentences and descriptive language in our reading **AF5**				
Heroes or Villains? **Date**	Back up our ideas in a discussion with evidence from the text **AF2**				
	Look at both sides of an argument and see the issues from more than one point of view **AF3**				
	Understand that the way authors present information sometimes shows us how they feel about a subject **AF6**				

PROJECT X – Guided reading targets and assessment record
BROWN BAND: STRONG DEFENCES

Book	Reading target We can ...	Name of child or group:			
		HIGH	SECURE	LOW	Comments
The X-bots are Coming **Date**	Use freeze frame to explore our understanding of stories **AF2/3**				
	Empathize with character's feelings and actions **AF3**				
	Discuss how authors create effects, including their choice of vocabulary **AF2/5**				
Attack of the X-bots! **Date**	Present a detailed account of an episode in the story, giving the events in the correct order **AF2**				
	Work out how characters feel from their words and actions **AF3**				
	Discuss how authors create effects, including their choice of vocabulary **AF2/5**				
Under Attack! **Date**	Debate issues using evidence from the text, listening carefully and responding to other people's points **AF2/3**				
	Make notes of the main points of sections of a text **AF2**				
	Use the context to work out the meaning of unfamiliar words **AF1**				
Lone Wolf **Date**	Discuss the story and reflect on it **AF2/3**				
	Work out how characters feel from their actions and empathize with them **AF2/3**				
	Identify descriptive language and discuss how it appeals to us **AF5**				
Strong Defences **Date**	Listen to and create a radio broadcast using appropriate presentational features **AF2**				
	Distinguish between the different kinds of texts in the book and say how they are organized **AF4**				
	Say which book we prefer and why **AF4/5**				

Project X – Self assessment sheet: Lime Band – Masks and Disguises

Name	
My reading targets	
I can talk about how characters feel and why	
I can draw conclusions about a character	
I can collect new words from my reading	
I can summarize the main points of a chapter or section in order	
I can identify descriptive language	

Project X – Self assessment sheet: Brown Band – Fast and Furious

Name	
My reading targets	
I can explain the main events of a story in a clear order	
I can identify descriptive language	
I can collect new words from my reading	
I can find ways in which a writer makes the reader react to a story	
I can talk about how characters are feeling about themselves and others	
I can give reasons for why I think something about my reading	
I can identify different features of a non-fiction text	

Project X – Self assessment sheet: Brown Band – Heroes and Villains

Name	
My reading targets	
I can work out how characters might be feeling and give reasons	
I can identify a moral dilemma in a story and talk about how I would feel	
I can talk about the words the author has used	
I can identify how a reference text is organized	
I can talk about the effect that different texts have on the reader	
I can identify and understand descriptive language	
I can look at an argument from more than one point of view	
I can understand how authors present different information	

Project X – Self assessment sheet: Brown Band – Strong Defences

Name	
My reading targets	
I can give a detailed account of part of a story	
I can work out how characters feel from their words and actions and empathize with them	
I can discuss how authors use words to create an affect on the reader	
I can debate issues using evidence from the text	
I can make notes to summarize the main points of a text	
I can identify descriptive language and say how it appeals to me	
I can distinguish between the different kinds of texts and say how they are organized	
I can say which book I prefer and why	

Comprehension Assessment Chart

This chart can be used at any point to assess the comprehension skills of a group or of an individual child.

√ = skills secure   / = not yet secure, more experience required

Name of child or group :	Dates:					
Comprehension Skill						
Uses prior knowledge						
Makes sensible predictions						
Supports predictions with evidence						
Confirms/changes predictions in the light of further reading						
Asks own questions of text						
Clarifies unknown vocabulary/ phrases/sentences						
Uses visualization techniques to enhance understanding						
Uses other sensory techniques to enhance understanding						
Retells sequentially						
Retells in detail						
Makes inferences from text/ illustrations						
Can deduce implicit information						
Can synthesize separate information						
Can summarize main points of story/ information text						
Identifies relevant/irrelevant material (determining importance)						
Identifies what has been learned						
Distinguishes between fact and opinion						
Draws conclusions						
Can empathize with characters/ behaviours						
Discusses author's point of view						
Discusses author's intentions						
Can take a critical stance to the text						
Makes personal responses						
Supports views with evidence from the text						
Reflection on Learning						
Can identify strategies used						
Can reflect on the effectiveness of strategies in supporting their understanding						

51

Reading Partners

Opportunities to read to a reading partner who has a similar reading ability can encourage children to share their success as a reader and undertake joint problem solving when they encounter difficulties. As the 'listener' has to follow the text as well, they too are practising their reading skills.

Reading partners should be encouraged to discuss the books they share – what they thought of them, what they learned, and any questions they have. This will help build a culture in which children see reading as a social and pleasurable activity. You could also encourage reading partners to share some of their discussion with the rest of the class.

You will need to model reading partner practice and talk through the prompt sheet [see page 53] before launching reading partnerships. Children should have a copy of the prompt sheet or you could enlarge it to A3 poster size and display.

Celebrating Achievement

With such an emphasis on targets and assessment it is important to children – as with any learner – that success is recognized and celebrated. Ongoing and informal praise of children's achievement is a key part of good teaching practice and guided or group reading sessions are an ideal time to focus on individual children. Children should also be encouraged to praise their peers and to identify and celebrate their own success.

On pages 54–55 you will find reading and writing certificate templates featuring the **Project X** characters. These can be used to celebrate the success of individuals or groups at any point in the school year.

Reading and Listening Partner Prompts

Before reading

Reader and listener:

- Look at the book together
- Talk about what you think it will be about

During reading

Listener:

- Listen really carefully
- Help your partner if they get stuck on a word

After reading

Reader and listener:

- Tell each other what you thought of the book
- What did you learn?
- What questions do you have?

Listener:

Tell your partner what you liked about their reading.

- Did they read with expression?
- Did they 'have a go' at hard words?

Reader and listener:

Decide if the reading was

- Fantastic
- Good
- A good try but need to practise and read again

Certificate for GREAT reading

has been awarded this certificate for

WELL DONE!

Signed: Max Cat Ant Tiger

Date:

Project X

Certificate for GREAT writing

has been awarded this certificate for

WELL DONE!

Signed: *Max Cat Ant Tiger*

Date:

Project X

Running Records

During your ongoing assessments of pupils you may identify a child who is falling behind their peers or who is failing to make progress at a particular point in time. Such children need a detailed, individual assessment of their reading strengths and weaknesses in order that you can identify the action needed to bring them back on track. A running record is a useful way to assess a child's reading strengths, areas for development, accuracy rate, error rate and self-correction rate.

As well as using running records to assess individual children at a point of specific need, they can also be used as regular progress checks. In particular, they are a useful way of helping you to assess and place children in appropriate guided reading groups.

Using the running record

Running records should be conducted with 'unseen' texts, so that they are a true assessment of a child's ability to read and interpret a new text. You can use any book at the appropriate level to undertake a running record. However on the following pages you will find one running record sample from a **Project X** book at each of the bands in Year 3/P4. If you choose to use these texts, you need to be aware of the samples and ensure you use them to undertake a running record before the child you wish to assess has encountered the text in a guided/group reading session.

You will need:

- A copy of the appropriate running record recording sheet for the reading level of the child (see pages 59–60)
- A copy of the book for the child to read from as you record
- A quiet space in which to conduct the assessment.

Before reading

- Explain to the child that you want to find out what they are doing well in their reading and where they might need a little bit more help. Stress that this is not a 'test'. Explain that you will be making some notes as they read so that you both can see what they did.
- Ask the child to read the piece of text aloud to you.

During reading

- Mark up your copy of the text as the child reads using the conventions shown on the reading behaviours chart opposite.
- Indicate whether the child used meaning/context (M), decoding (ph), structure/syntax (S) or visual cues (V)
  in working out new or unfamiliar words.
- Also record what strategies the child used in self-correcting errors.
- If the child struggles with a word give them plenty of time to try out different ways of identifying the word. Avoid the temptation to instantly prompt them as you want to assess what the child can do unaided. When it is clear that the child is not going to read the word unaided you can then offer prompts or give the word.

After reading

- Give the child some immediate positive feedback e.g. look, here you said the wrong word but you realized it was wrong and then you corrected the mistake. Well done.
- Ask the child to summarize what they have read and ask them a few questions to informally assess their overall understanding. Include questions that require recall, inference and deduction.

Running Records – Reading Behaviours Chart

Child's reading behaviour	How to record	Example
Child reads accurately (no error)	√ Tick each correct word	√ √ √ √ √ Every cloud has a silver
Child substitutes another word (counts as one error even if several different words tried)	Write final substituted word above the word	√ car √ √ √ Every cloud has a silver
Child self-corrected substitution (no error)	Write SC after substitution to indicate self-corrected	√ car/SC √ √ √ Every cloud has a silver
Child omits a word (one error)	Write a long dash above the word	√ √ √ – √ Every cloud has a silver
Child inserts a word (one error)	Write ^ at point of insertion and the word inserted	√ little √ √ √ √ Every ^ cloud has a silver
Child corrects repetition of a word or phrase (no error)	Write R1 (one repetition), R2 (two repetitions) etc above word. If a phrase is repeated underline the phrase.	√ R2 √ √ √ Every cloud has a silver
Child sounds out all or part of a word (no error if correct; one error if word given by teacher)	Mark the sounds used and write √ if word correct or G if word given	√ c l /ow/d√ √ √ √ Every cloud has a silver
Teacher prompting: Child stops after one attempt and does not try again – teacher prompts them to have another go (one error)	Write TP above the word then √ if word read correctly or G if word then given	√ TP√ √ √ √ Every cloud has a silver √ TP/G √ √ √ Every cloud has a silver
Teacher intervention: Child makes no attempt to read the word (one error)	Write G above the word if child is given the word after a 5-10 second wait	√ G √ √ √ Every cloud has a silver

Analysing the running record

It is best to undertake the detailed analysis of a running record immediately after a session while it is still fresh in your mind.

Your analysis should follow this basic format:

1. Note your general comments about the child's reading and understanding of the text.
2. Note the number of errors and self-corrections.
3. Look at the types of cues and strategies the child used during errors and self correcting:
   - Are they over-dependent on one particular cue?
   - Are there any cues they are not using?
   - Was the child confident to attempt words they were finding difficult?
   - Is there any repeated pattern of errors e.g. a particular word/phoneme?
4. Reflect on what this tells you about the child's strengths and areas for development.
5. Note the child's specific needs and ideas for further experiences in the next steps box.

Numerical analysis

You may also wish to undertake a numerical analysis of the running record using the first 100 words of the sample text, as follows:

Self-correction rate

A child's self-correction rate is expressed as a ratio and is calculated using the following formula:

$$\frac{(E + SC)}{SC} = SC \text{ rate} \qquad \frac{(\text{Errors} + \text{self-corrections})}{\text{self-corrections}} = \text{self-correction rate}$$

Example:

$$\frac{(10 + 5)}{5} = SC \qquad \frac{15}{5} = SC \qquad 3 = SC$$

The SC rate is 1:3. This means that the child corrects 1 out of every 3 errors.

If a child has a self-correcting rate of 1:3 or less, this indicates that they are successfully self-monitoring their reading. A higher ratio (1:4 and above) indicates that the child needs more support in reading for meaning.

Accuracy rate

A child's accuracy rate is expressed as a percentage and is calculated using the following formula:

$$\frac{(\text{Total words read} - \text{total errors})}{\text{Total words read}} \times 100 = \text{Accuracy rate}$$

Example:

$$\frac{(110 - 6)}{110} \times 100 = AR \qquad \frac{104}{110} \times 100 = AR \qquad 94\% = AR$$

The accuracy rate indicates the level of difficulty of the text for the reader as follows:

Accuracy Rate	Text level
95–100%	Easy enough for independent reading
90–94%	Guided reading instructional level
Below 90%	Too difficult – frustration level for independent reading

Running record sheet 1

Name of child:	BOOK BAND 11: LIME
	BOOK TITLE: SHARKS ON THE LOOSE!
Date:	

Symbols:
√ = correct   SC = self-corrected   – = word omitted
^ = word inserted   TP = Teacher prompt   G = given

Strategies used:
M = meaning (context)   V = visual   Ph = decoding   S = structure/syntax

As you mark up the text you should assess the strategy the child uses e.g. self-correcting may involve using meaning or sentence structure or both. If two strategies are used together enclose these in a circle.

The sharks saw their prey	Type of strategy
They waited and watched as the group of children moved closer and closer. The sharks' hungry eyes looked for a chance to attack. The children stayed packed together, like a shoal of sardines. Then one kid waved her arm. The sharks' eyes lit up.	
Yes, there would be blood.	
Yes, there would be screams.	
The sharks knew there would be no mercy. They'd attack at speed and then vanish before they could be caught.	
No one would ever know what happened.	
No one would ever find them.	
Time to move in.	
Time to attack ...	
Total words: 100	

General comment on reading and understanding
Use of reading cues

Self-correction rate

Accuracy rate

Next steps

Running record sheet 2

Name of child:	BOOK BAND 12: BROWN
	BOOK TITLE: THE CHASE
Date:	

Symbols:

√ = correct   SC = self-corrected   − = word omitted

^ = word inserted   TP = Teacher prompt   G = given

Strategies used:

M = meaning (context)   V = visual   Ph = decoding   S = structure/syntax

As you mark up the text you should assess the strategy the child uses e.g. self-correcting may involve using meaning or sentence structure or both. If two strategies are used together enclose these in a circle.

	Type of strategy
It was a hot summer's day and the children had been playing in the park. Tiger was snoozing in the cool shade of a tree. He dreamed that someone was tickling his wrist. It was really quite a nice feeling. Then he opened his eyes. He knew straight away that something was wrong. Tiger looked around him. He could see Max and Cat chatting. Max was showing Cat his new skateboard. Ant was also close by, reading a book. He was always reading. Tiger sometimes made fun of him, but he knew deep down that reading was cool. His friends were all fine. So what was it then? Why did he feel so strange?	
Total words: 114	

General comment on reading and understanding

Use of reading cues

Self-correction rate

Accuracy rate

Next steps

Reading at home – working with parents/carers

Parents and/or carers are children's first and continuing teachers. It is well known that parents who regularly read with and to their children, and who act as good 'model readers' themselves, play a vital role in children's development as readers.

A home or care situation in which a wide variety of reading material – books, magazines, newspapers, the internet, and so on – is seen and valued as a part of every day life makes a huge difference to children's attitudes to reading.

Of course, not all home backgrounds provide these 'ideal' conditions. Some parents/carers may need your support to become actively involved in helping their child understand the pleasures and purposes of reading. It is important, too, to be sensitive to those parents/carers for whom English is not a first language (or indeed, where English isn't spoken at all) or who may struggle with literacy themselves.

Your approach to parent or carer needs will, to some extent, depend on your individual school situation. But whatever the circumstances, the vast majority of parents do want to help their children learn and there are many exciting and innovative ways schools can encourage this. You could, for example:

- Have reading induction meetings where you explain how parents/carers can help with reading, role play 'hearing a child read' and show a range of literacy resources that involve enjoyable reading activities.
- Offer parents, or loan out to parents, the NIACE/Basic Skills Agency family literacy resources such as *Read and Write Together*, *Learning with Grandparents*, *Fun at home*, *Fun outdoors* and so on. See http://archive.basic-skills.co.uk/
- Involve children and parents/carers in national projects such as Dads and Lads, Reading Champions, Family Learning Week and so on.
- Arrange special family induction trips to the local library or arrange for the mobile library to come to the school playground once a week.
- Involve parents/carers in creating Story Sacks and Curiosity Kits – fiction and non-fiction book bags with related artefacts and toys – to use in the home.
- Have a library of reading games that can be taken home to play.
- Have family quiz events to generate discussion and enthusiasm around reading, or create a supermarket word trail.
- Involve parents/carers in celebrating events such as World Book Day, Children's Book Week, National Storytelling Week, National Poetry Day and so on.
- Run your own book awards event and have parent/carer votes as well as children's.
- Run a regular 'book swap' stall where both parents and children can swap books, comics and magazines.

Inside the cover of each **Project X** book are notes for parents/carers that point out tricky vocabulary, encourage talk about books, and suggest some fun activities that parents/carers and children can enjoy together.

Opposite you will find a sheet of simple tips and practical advice for parents/carers on how to support their child with their reading. This can be photocopied or adapted for your own Home-School programme.

Reading with your child

Here are some simple tips to help you help your child with reading

Enjoy it!

- Make book sharing a fun time that you both enjoy – snuggle up with a book!
- When your child reads to you, show them that you are proud of what they can do.
- Even though your child has started to read it's still important that you read to them. Read them old favourites – even if they do seem 'easy' – as well as longer or harder books that they can't manage themselves.
- If you have a shared interest or hobby, look at books and magazines on the topic together.

Make time and space!

- Make reading a special part of your day. Try to find a time when you aren't busy doing other things so you can spend 'quality time' reading together – even if it's only for a few minutes.
- Try to find a quiet place away from distractions like the television or the computer.
- Try to find some time every day for reading together – 10 to 15 minutes each day is better than a long session once a week.
- If your child is reluctant to read you could offer a small reward such as playing a game they enjoy. If they are tired or very reluctant to read to you, read to them instead. Don't force them.

Be positive!

- Give your child lots praise, encouragement and support when they read to you. Focus on what they did well, not what they did wrong. Even small successes are important.

Find out what they like to read!

- Sometimes we read for pleasure but most of the time we read for a reason. Read lots of different things together – stories, information books, comics, magazines, websites, cereal packets, TV listings – anything you and your child enjoy reading or need to read.
- Let your child make his or her own reading choices sometimes. They need to develop their own personal likes and dislikes. It is OK not to like some books! Don't worry if they choose an 'easy' or favourite book over and over again. This is normal and helps children build their reading confidence and enthusiasm.
- Join the local library and let your child choose from the great range of books on offer.

Talk about it!

- Talking about books will help your child become more involved and interested in reading and can help them understand more.
- After you've read a book together – or anything else you choose to read – talk about it. What was it about? How did it make you feel? What did you like or not like about it? What did you learn? Spend some time looking at the pictures and talk about what they tell you. Never cover the pictures while sharing a book.
- You can talk with your child about anything – games, TV programmes, films or other things you do together.

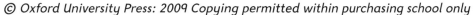

Project X – Using a thematic approach

Over the last few years more and more primary schools have begun to move away from teaching all curriculum subjects in separate slots in the timetable to one where some subjects are linked together in cross-curricular 'themes'. The Primary National Strategy, through various initiatives, has supported this approach, while stressing that links should be strong and meaningful, not tenuous.

Making links between curriculum subjects can deepen children's understanding by providing opportunities to enhance their learning. It does this in a number of ways.

- It mirrors the way we learn 'naturally', outside school – our learning environment is often holistic, for example, going shopping might involve literacy, maths and geography.

- It builds and enriches concepts – by presenting the same or related information in different ways, through different modes of communication or within different contexts.

- It provides opportunities for the application of knowledge within familiar, new and related contexts and supports children in using higher order thinking skills such as reasoning and problem solving.

- It provides opportunities for practising skills – so, skills taught in one curriculum area (e.g. skimming, scanning and analyzing data in literacy) can be developed through purposeful use in other areas such as history or science.

- It helps children retain their learning through the repetition of information, actions and skills in different contexts.

- It makes learning enjoyable – cross-curricular learning often feels more meaningful and more fun, so motivation and engagement can be enhanced.

In using cross-curricular themes it is important to recognize that planning is still usually undertaken at subject level to ensure curriculum coverage and continuity. For this reason the cross-curricular potential of the themes in **Project X** are linked to the National Curriculum Programmes of Study. The grids on pages 65-68 contain suggestions for many activities linked to the wider curriculum, as well as ideas for creating a contextualised learning environment which will encourage children to make their own explorations of a theme through play and other activities. Such activities also encourage them to make direct links between the theme and their own knowledge and experiences.

At each Book Band level **Project X** offers five books linked by a theme. This cluster structure is designed to support a cross-curricular approach and to be motivating and engaging for readers.

Project X-Lime Band- Theme: Masks and Disguises

Cross-curricular opportunities – Theme: Masks and Disguises

The learning environment

- Have a range of masks for children to handle and /or wear. Include masks from different world cultures, masks found in modern and historical periods, masks for different purposes.
- Have a box of stage make-up, wigs, false beards and so on so that children can experiment with creating fictional identities and disguises. Many theatre companies will offer stage make-up demonstrations for schools.
- Create a stage 'dressing room' as a role play area. Include make-up and dressing up resources.
- Provide plenty of story books and other reading or multimedia materials involving characters using masks and disguises – traditional tales and myths provide many examples, as do modern detective stories and superhero adventures. Include non-fiction materials on subjects such as secret agents, spies, acting, and the use of masks for protection.

National Curriculum subject	Programme of study	Suggested activities
Science	Sc2 Life processes and living things 5. Living things in their environment/ adaptation c) how animals/plants are adapted to their environment	Look at animal camouflage for different environments/habits/life cycles. Consider the importance of appearance and camouflage/ disguise for animals and plants. (Link to issues explored in *Stage Fright*)
Art and design Maths Music Dance (PE)	Art and Design: Breadth of study a) Exploring a range of starting points for practical work b) Working on their own and with others on projects in 2D and 3D Maths 3: Space shape and measure 2. Understanding properties of shape c) make and draw 2D and 3D shapes and patterns Music: breadth of study a) musical activities that integrate performing, composing and appraising PE: Dance activities a) create and perform dances using a range of movement patterns including those from different times, places and cultures	Look at masks from a range of cultures and purposes such as tribal masks or theatrical masks. (You could link to animal camouflage or to a historical period being studied). Look at their symmetrical/asymmetrical properties, use of pattern, colour and materials. Design, draw and make a mask. Use the masks in a dance drama sequence, creating appropriate music to accompany the dance, e.g. African masks with drumming music. Review and appraise their work. (Link to *Sharks on the Loose!*, *Safe Behind a Mask* and *Masks in Film and Theatre*)
History/ICT	4. Historical enquiry Find out about events and people from an appropriate range of sources of information including ICT based sources ICT: Breadth of study Working with others to explore a variety of information sources and ICT tools	Look at the use of masks/disguises in an historical context, e.g. Greek theatre, the wooden horse of Troy, gods adopting disguises, funeral masks in ancient Egypt, gas masks in World War II … (Link to *Safe Behind a Mask*)
DT	Knowledge, skills and understanding Designing, making and evaluating All process stages 1-3	Explore a variety of puppets – shadow, hand, string, paper bag etc. Make puppets to enact a traditional story where disguise is involved e.g. wolf disguised as grandma, fairy disguised as old women, prince disguised as a beast and so on. (Link to *Masks in Film and Theatre*)
PSHE / citizenship/ Geography	4. Developing good relationships and respecting the differences between people b) Think about the lives of people in other places …different customs 3. Developing a healthy safer lifestyle	Discuss the use of masks, costumes and veils in different cultures. Discuss the safety aspects of masks (including helmets and visors) and why they are important. (Link to *Masks in Film and Theatre* and *Safe Behind a Mask*)

Cross-curricular opportunities – Theme: Fast and Furious

The learning environment

- Small world play/experimentation could include a race track and model vehicles.
- Create a role play area in the form of the mechanics 'pit' on a racetrack. Provide examples of and/or encourage children to create e.g. safety posters, log books, car manuals, tyre pressure charts, racing league tables, lap times and so on.
- Create or provide indoor and outdoor games that involve racing – you could even organize your own charity fun run, creating a route, sponsorship forms etc
- Provide books, magazines, DVDs and other materials about fast people, vehicles and animals.
- Display examples of art works showing 'speed' such as futurist movement paintings.

National Curriculum subject	Programme of study	Suggested activities
Science	*Sc4 Physical Process* Force and motion 2c-e Friction, pushes and pulls, measuring forces/direction *Sc2 Life Processes* 2h) the importance of exercise for good health	Set up a series of fair tests to determine the speed of different toy vehicles on a variety of surfaces. Adjust the surfaces to provide more or less friction. Chart and compare results and draw conclusions. (Link to *Top Speed*, *The Super Skateplank* and *Downhill Racers*) Explore the effects of exercise on the human body. (Link to *The Fun Run*)
Geography	*3 Knowledge and understanding of places* a) identify and describe what places are like e) explain why places are like they are *Geographical enquiry and skills* 2e) to draw maps and plans	Explore local/national rail, road and air routes. Create maps showing local transport routes including bus routes, cycle paths and footpaths. Undertake a local traffic survey to see which is the quickest means of transport for the local area. (Link to *The Chase* and *Top Speed*)
D/T	*Knowledge, skills and understanding* Designing, making and evaluating All process stages 1-3	Design and make a streamlined moving vehicle. (Link to *Top Speed* and *Downhill Racers*)
Music	*Breadth of study* d) A range of live and recorded music from different times and cultures b) Responding to a range of musical starting points	Explore ways of representing speed and motion in music, e.g. in Enigma variations, film soundtracks during chase scenes, African drumming with increasing tempo and so on. Create own speed music linked to a story. (Link to *The Super Skateplank* and *The Chase*)
History	*2 Knowledge and understanding of changes in the past* d) Describe and make links between the main events, situations and changes within and across different periods	Explore the development of transport from horse drawn to modern motor cars, planes, trains etc. Discuss how the need for speed has impacted on the development of transport. Alternatively, focus on the development of one means of transport such as the bicycle. (Link to *Top Speed*)
Art and design /ICT	*4 Knowledge and understanding* a) Visual and tactile elements including colour, pattern and texture, line and tone, shape, form and space and how these elements are combined and organized for different purposes	Explore ways of representing speed and motion in art. Use digital photographs and take images of children moving at speed. Use swirls and other digital effects to create an image of movement. (Link to *The Super Skateplank* and *The Chase*)
PE/mathematics	*10 Athletic activities* a) take part in and design challenges that call for precision speed, power or stamina b) use running skills	Design and undertake a series of individual and team running activities. Record and chart times and distances. Keep an exercise diary. (Link to *The Fun Run*)
PSHE /citizenship /mathematics	*3. Developing a healthy, safer life style*	Collect transport to school and journey time statistics. Make charts. Discuss speed aspects of different vehicles versus health and environmental issues. Discuss the safety aspects of all journey types.

Cross-curricular opportunities – Theme: Heroes and Villains

The learning environment

- Small world play could include superhero action figures, vehicles, buildings and construction toys so that children can create their own imaginary worlds for enacting 'goodie v baddie' stories and scenarios.
- Provide dressing up materials, masks, capes etc so that children can play the part of their favourite heroes and villains.
- Create a role play area based on an emergency services HQ – with telephones, maps, job lists, emergency drills and procedures etc.
- Display posters showing emergency services at work and other local community 'heroes' such as crossing patrol workers and so on.
- Provide a range of fiction and non-fiction books, comics, audio and video material relating to the theme of heroes and villains. There are lots of examples from classic literature, traditional tales and modern media.
- Arrange a visit from the local air ambulance team, coastguard, fire brigade or other emergency service.

National Curriculum subject	Programme of study	Suggested activities
Science/history	*Sc1 scientific enquiry* a) that science is about thinking creatively to try to explain how living and non-living things work and to establish links between causes and effects	Investigate scientific heroes/heroines. Look at the work of a significant scientist, related to the area of science area being explored. (Link to *Heroes or Villains?*)
Art and design	*Breadth of study* a) Exploring a range of starting points *2 Investigating and making* c) use a variety of methods and approaches to communicate ideas and feelings and to design and make images	Look at examples of art works which make everyday workers look heroic. Design a poster celebrating everyday heroes in the community. Explore how comic book hero and villain conventions are used in pop-art and in films. (Link to *Dr X's Top 10 Villains* and *Jake Jones v Vlad the Bad*)
Music	*4 Listening and applying knowledge and understanding* d) how music is used for particular purposes *2 Creating and developing musical ideas*	Explore how music is used in films, TV programmes, cartoons and on computer games to signal heroes and villains. (Link to *Dr X's Top 10 Villains*) Create a story board and some hero and villain music to accompany key scenes from a story. (Link to *Heroine in Hiding*, *Air Scare* and *Jake Jones v Vlad the Bad*)
History/ICT	*4 Historical enquiry* a) How to find out about events and people from a range of sources of information including ICT *Breadth of study - local history study* *ICT 1 Finding things out* a) gather information from a variety of sources	Research the histories of people/animals who have received awards for bravery. Look particularly for any local examples. Use internet search engines as a starting point and share the outcomes of the research using a multimedia presentation or by creating a class biographical dictionary. Make a class *Top 10 Heroes book*. Contrast with *Dr X's Top 10 Villains*
D/T	*Knowledge, skills and understanding* *Designing, making and evaluating* All process stages 1-3	Research transportation devices for superheroes and/or villains. Design a transportation system for a superhero or villain. Include design notes explaining the features and what they enable the hero/villain to do. (Link to *Dr X's Top 10 Villains*, *Heroine in Hiding* and *Jake Jones v Vlad the Bad*)
PSHE / citizenship	*4 Developing good relationships* e) to recognize and challenge stereotypes	Look at the stereotypical images/characteristics of heroes/heroines in traditional stories. Discuss stereotypical gender images. Challenge some of the stereotypes through discussion and comparison with different examples.

Cross-curricular opportunities – Theme: Strong Defences

The learning environment

- Small world play could include model castles and forts; provide a range of construction materials that can be used to create strong defences, such as castles, siege engines, walls etc
- Create a role play area on a castle theme, providing dressing up resources and writing materials so that children can plan out and enact their defence strategies
- Display plans, posters, books and DVDs of castles and other defensive structures, including animal defences
- A display of defensive sports equipment such as knee pads, face guards, helmets etc could be created
- Provide a range of story and non-fiction books, audio and video material relating to the theme of strong defences – myths and legends provide many good examples.

National Curriculum subject	Programme of study	Suggested activities
Science	Sc2 Life processes 5 Living things in their environment a) The way living things need protection f) Micro-organisms	Explore different types of animal defences, e.g. animals that live in shells, structures built, habits/lifestyle. Look at how different animals look after their young. (Link to *Lone Wolf* and *Strong Defences*) Explore germs and bacteria - grow moulds (taking suitable health and safety precautions). (Link to *Strong Defences*)
	Sc3 Materials and their properties I Grouping and classifying materials	Test the properties of different materials and decide which would be most suitable to build a defensive structure and why. (You could use *The Three Little Pigs* as a starting point here.) (Link to *The X-bots are Coming*, *Attack of the X-bots* and *Under Attack!*)
D/T Maths /ICT	Knowledge, skills and understanding Designing, making and evaluating All process stages 1-3 MA3 Measures MA4 Handling Data ICT 3 Exchanging and Sharing information a) share/exchange information in a variety of ways b) Be sensitive to needs of audience	Design a siege machine or a castle with a working drawbridge. Design and make a trebuchet. Measure the distances/angles an object can be thrown by a trebuchet. Record distances of different throws in graphs. Make a sandcastle and use small world play figures to create stop-frame animated 'documentary' on attack/defence. (Link to *Attack of the X-bots*, *Strong Defences* and *Under Attack!*)
PSHE/ICT	3 Developing a healthy, safer life style	Discuss sensible precautions for staying safe including e.g. being safe on the Internet, mobile phone bullying
PE	2 Selecting and applying skills and tactics	Explore defensive and attack strategies in various team games, e.g. netball, football, etc
History	4 Historical Enquiry 2 Knowledge and understanding of events, people and changes in the past	Research castles and their defences – or other defensive structures linked to the period of historical study, e.g. Roman forts/Hadrian's wall
Geography	Geographical enquiry and skills I Developing geographical skills 2 d-e	Identify the features of defensive sites and the reasons for the siting of specific defensive structures in the locality – e.g. on high ground, by water etc (Link to *Under Attack!* and *Strong Defences*)

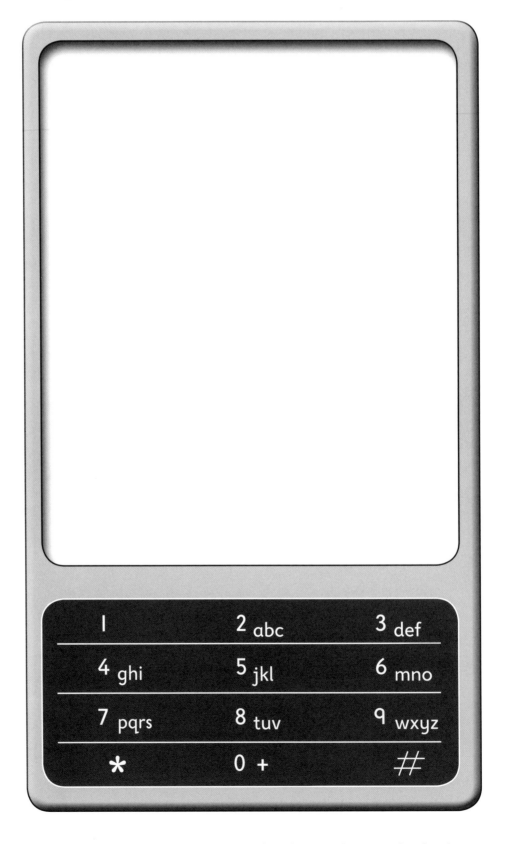

Name ....

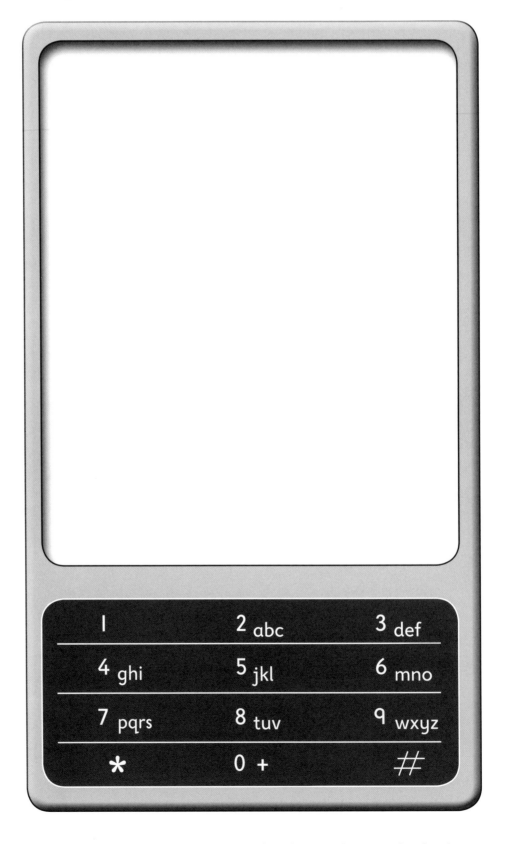

Warning!

Compose a text message to one of the gang to warn them about the Phoney Mob.

Name ....

Stage Fright – Inference grid

Read each section from chapter 3 and write down what you can infer from the information. The first one has been done for you.

Chapter 3	This makes me think that …
In a secret underground hideout, a man in a purple suit was watching a screen.	The man is spying on someone.
Behind him were two other men, one short, one tall. They were wearing dark grey suits. They were called Plug and Socket.	
"Aha!" exclaimed Dr X. "This could be the chance we've been waiting for to get the watches back."	
"Continue monitoring the situation. I have to go out."	
(Plug says:) "What does *monitoring the situation* mean?" "Just watch the screen, nitwit," Dr X replied. "Oh is something good on?"	

Name ....

Masks in Film and Theatre KWL grid

What I know about masks	What I would like to find out about masks	What I learned about masks

Project X

Name ....

4

Masks in Film and Theatre summary

Make notes about each section in *Masks in Film and Theatre*.
The first section has been done for you.

Section title	Main points of the section
Dressing up	Masks and costumes used for hundreds of years Masks change a person's looks and feelings Actors can pretend to be someone or something else
Masks in theatre	
Carnival time	
Bring on the clowns!	
Film and TV make-up	
Digital masks	

Name ....

Leo and Matt's town map

Use the story and the pictures to create a map of the town where Leo and Matt live.

Make up a name for the town to make it more interesting!

Map of _____

Key

Project X: Lime band – Masks and Disguises – Sharks on the Loose

Name ....

Help Felini's Fantastic Fish Bar

Design a poster to persuade people to visit Felini's Fantastic Fish Bar. Think carefully about how you will:

- persuade people to visit (You could use special offers.)
- present the words
- make the poster eye-catching.

_____

Special Offers

Project X: Lime band – Masks and Disguises – Sharks on the Loose

Name ....

Purposes of masks

Write down the purpose and any special features of some of the masks in *Safe Behind a Mask*. The first one has been done for you.

Type of mask	Protection or disguise?	Purpose	Special features					
Plague doctor's mask	Protection	Protect themselves against bad air	Goggles to protect the eyes Beak filled with herbs					

Project X: Lime-band – Masks and Disguises – Safe Behind a Mask

Name ....

Superhero costume

Use the body outline to create a costume for a superhero.
Think about:
- what sort of superpowers your hero will have
- the costume your hero will need, e.g. wings, fire-resistant cloth

Label the diagram carefully with your hero's special features.

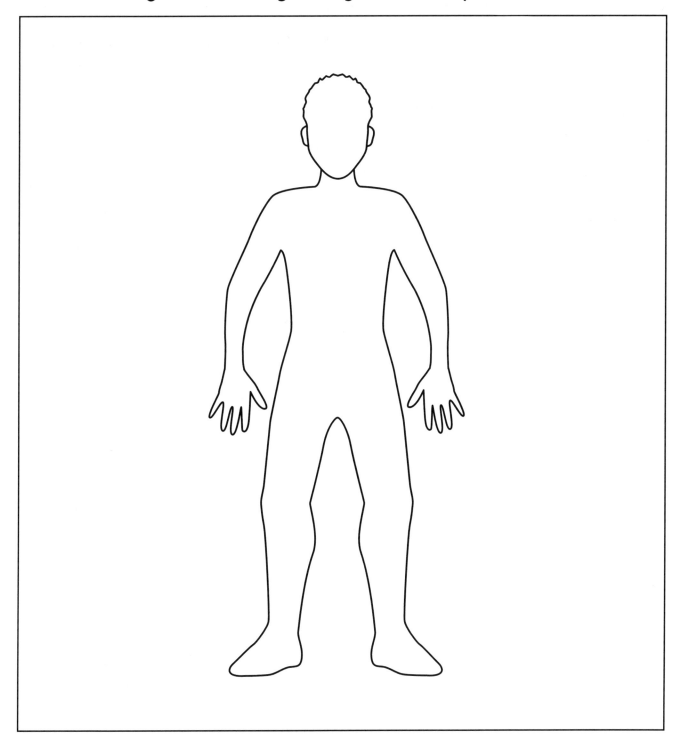

Name ....

Vocabulary cards

contraption	contraption	unzipped	unzipped
frantically	frantically	grimaced	grimaced
tickling	tickling	**covering**	**covering**
screeched	screeched	anxiously	anxiously
realized	**realized**	gathered	gathered
unfastened	unfastened	**brilliant**	**brilliant**
desperately	desperately	reluctantly	reluctantly
whirled	whirled	lowering	lowering
precisely	**precisely**	hovering	hovering
nervously	nervously	**weaving**	**weaving**
hurriedly	hurriedly	reflection	reflection
concentrating	concentrating	**splattered**	splaterred

Name ....

Email

Write an email to a local runner or famous athlete to invite him or her to take part in your fun run.

To:	
cc:	
Subject:	
Message:	

Project X: Brown band – Fast and Furious – The Fun Run

Name ....

Exercise diary

○ Date...........................

○ Exercise carried out:

○ _____

○ _____

○ _____

○ _____

○ _____

○ _____

○ Time taken for exercise:

○ _____

○ _____

○ _____

○ _____

○ What I ate today:

○ _____

○ _____

○ _____

○ _____

○ _____

○ _____

Name ....

Racer rankings

Rank the riders from *Downhill Racers* in their world ranking order. You may have to find more information on the AGSA website before you can complete this chart.

Name of rider	World ranking	Personal best

Name ....

Emotions grid

Write words to say how Ben is feeling in each chapter. Remember to start with the low, sad feelings at the bottom and the high, happy feelings at the top.

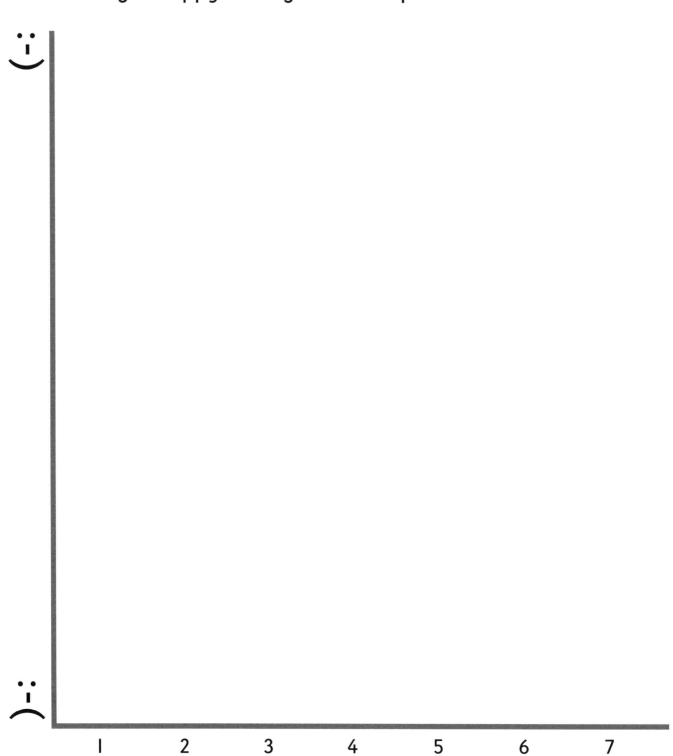

Chapter

Name ....

Story plan

Plan a short story about the day you entered a
competition, or the day you lost something important.

Main characters	Opening
Problem/Dilemma	**Resolution**

Really good vocabulary I want to use

Project X: Brown band – Fast and Furious – The Super Skateplank

Name ....

Speed: For and against

Use this chart to record information for and against the use of speed.

Section	For	Against

Name ....

Newspaper

Use this outline to write your article about a speed event.

Headline: *(capture their attention)*	
Opening paragraph: *(outline main event, when and where it happened)*	**Photograph:**
Sub headline:	**Caption:**
Details of event: *(describe what happened)*	**Final paragraph:** *(outcome of event and details of future events)*

Name ....

Spot the difference

Have another look at the diagrams of the Whizzer (page 2-3) and Air Shark (page 10-11). Then use the chart below to note the differences between them. Use technical vocabulary wherever you can.

THE WHIZZER	AIR SHARK

Name ....

Top secret invention

Details of the X-POD/X-BOT
Only for sharing with other expert scientists from NASTI

Diagram:

Notes to help you answer other scientists' questions about the invention.

-

-

-

Name ....

Dr X's Top 10 Villains summary

Can you complete the chart?

Name	Story/film/comic/game	Nasty characteristics	DR X's RATING	MY RATING
Darth Vader	Star Wars		1	
Davros				
Dr Octopus				
The White Witch				
The Joker				
He-Who-Must-Not-Be-Named				
Lex Luthor				

Project X: Brown band – Heroes and Villains – Dr X's Top 10 Villains

Name ....

Villain profile

Create your own villain profile using the table below.

NAME OF VILLAIN	
SPECIES	
BIRTH PLACE	
OTHER NAMES	
BASE	
MISSION	
STRENGTHS	
WEAKNESSES	

Name ....

Code breakers

Can you read these messages? Work out the code and then write a reply using the same code.

Dr Jk,
Vld th Bd s gng t strk tmrrw aftrnn.
Mt m tnght t th HQ t mk plns.
Brng th trnsmttr.
Dnt lt Vlt knw.
Hrry Hndsm

Your reply

Can you work out this code? (There's a clue at the bottom of the page if you get stuck)

Up Ibssz,
Uifsf't b qspcmfn xjui uif TqzTdppufs.
J xjmm offe up hfu ju gjyfe cfgpsf J dbo nffu zpv.
Kblf

Your reply

CLUE TO CRACK THE CODE: Change each letter to the one which comes before it in the alphabet. Eg j=i

Name ....

Hero or villain?

On page 30 it says that often what the media gives us is an opinion but what we really need are facts.

Choose a person from the book – or someone else you know a lot about – and decide what is a fact and what is opinion from all the things you have found out about them.

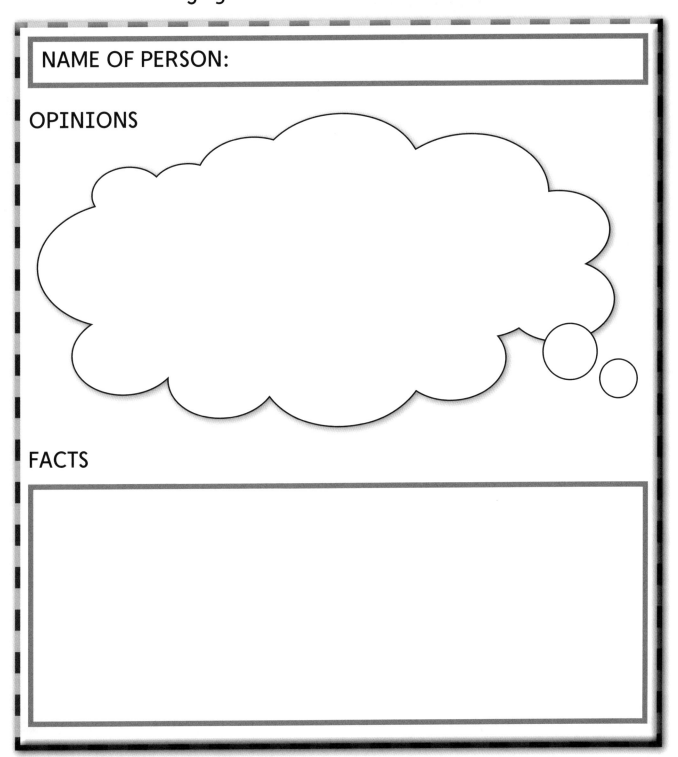

NAME OF PERSON:

OPINIONS

FACTS

Project X: Brown band – Heroes and Villains – Heroes or Villains?

Name ....

Den locations

Fill in the advantages and disadvantages for each den location.

Location	Advantages	Disadvantages
Tree stump	• Already familiar	
Branch of a tree		• Ant afraid of heights
Island	• Provides a ready built moat	

Castle for sale

Write an advertisement for the castle on the island.

UNIQUE OPPORTUNITY
PRIVATE CASTLE FOR SALE

Picture of the castle.

Location: Rooms:

Additional features:

Grounds:

Name ....

Problems and outcomes

Write notes to show what action resulted from each problem. The first one has been done for you.

Problem encountered by the X-bots	Action/result
Pond	X-bots open inflatable rubber rings. Can float across pond.
Pike	
Water catapult	
Bubblegum trap	
Magnet trap	
Castle walls	
Ducks	

Project X: Brown band – Strong Defences – Attack of the X-bots!

Name ....

Note-taking frame

Make notes as you read each section of *Under Attack*.

Type of defence	Why it is useful	Example
Water		
Walls		
Weapons and traps		
Alarms		
Security cameras		

Project X: Brown band – Strong Defences – Under Attack!

Name ....

Wolf words

Write words relating to wolves around the wolf.

Project X: Brown band – Strong Defences – Lone Wolf

Name ....

Timeline of Grey's awful day

Write about the events in Grey's bad day in the box below. The first one has been done for you.

Morning	Afternoon	Evening
Plaging with family outside den		

Name ....

Character profile

Draw a picture of the character then make notes about them.

| Appearance |
| Family |
| Likes |
| Dislikes |
| Personality |

Name ....

Character log

Create your own character. Make notes about them to help you.

I am ...
I live ...
I have ...
I like ...
I don't like ...
Anything else?

Name ....

Character relationships grid

Use this grid to record the relationships between different characters in a story. Write in the names of the characters. Make notes in each box to show character relationships (e.g. mother/son) and what the characters think of each other.

Book title:

Author:

	Character 1	Character 2	Character 3	Character 4
Character 1				
Character 2				
Character 3				
Character 4				

Name ....

Prediction and reflection grid

What do you think might happen in the book?
Make notes in the first two columns before you read the book.
What did happen in the book? Make notes in the last column after reading.

Book title Author		
I think this might happen ...	I think this because ...	What did happen

Name ....

Inference grid

After reading a book, think about what you know and what you learned.

| **Book title** |
| **Author** |
| **What I know about from reading the book** |
| |
| **What I know about from clues in the book and my own thinking** (Think about what you can work out from the words not just what the words say.) |
| |

Name ....

Synthesizing grid (1 + 1 = 2)

Use this chart to help you make links between the information in different parts of a book. What new information do you find by adding up the facts?

| Book title | | |
Author		
I found this out on page …	I found this out on page …	These two things together tell me …
I found this out on page …	I found this out on page …	These two things together tell me …
I found this out on page …	I found this out on page …	These two things together tell me …

Name ....

Think, feel, say ...

During or after reading a book, make notes in the shapes below to help you form an opinion.

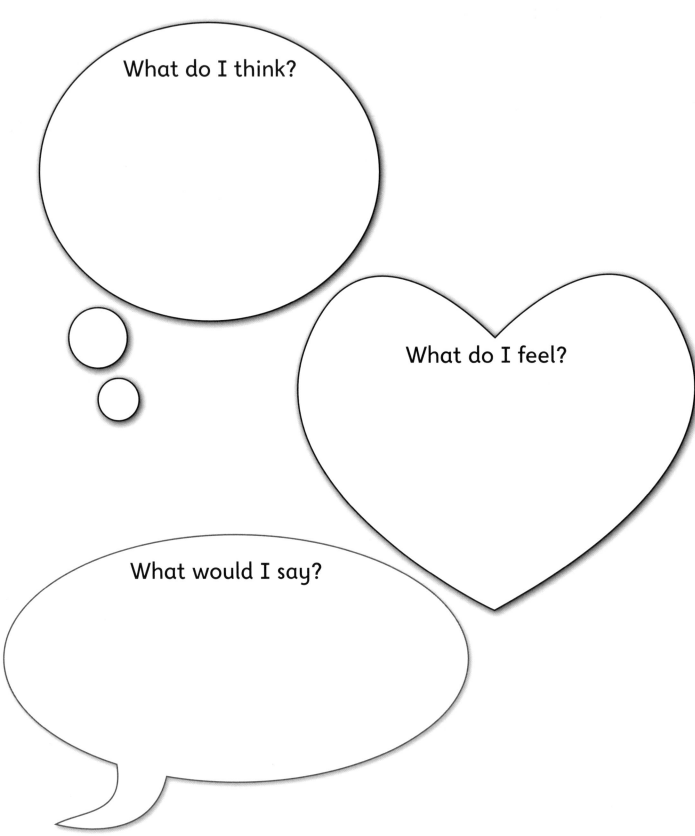

What do I think?

What do I feel?

What would I say?

Name ....

See, think, wonder ...

Make notes about an episode in a story. What can you see?
What does it make you think? What might happen next?

I see ...

I wonder ...

I think ...

Name ....

Cause and effect

Use these tables to record events and their effects.

Fiction

CAUSE	EFFECT
What did the character do?	What happened because of this?
What is the event?	What happened as a result?

Non-fiction

CAUSE	EFFECT
What is the event?	What happened as a result?
What is the step in the process?	What happened as a result?

Name ....

Compare and contrast information

Use this grid to compare and contrast information from different non-fiction sources – e.g. books, magazines, video clips, the internet.

Information source 1	Information source 2	Information source 3
Title:	Title:	Title:
What I found out ...	What I found out ...	What I found out ...

Name ....

Before and after reading

Use this grid to compare what you know before reading a book with what you know after reading.

Statement	Before reading			After reading		
	True ✓	False X	Don't know ?	True ✓	False X	Don't know ?

Name ....

Word detective

Use this sheet to record new words you meet when reading.
List the word and its meaning.

Book title	
Author	
New word	**Word meaning**

Name ....

Story board

Use this story board to help you when planning a story.

Characters

Setting

What happens at the beginning?

What happens in the middle?

What happens at the end?

Name ....

Note taking

Use this grid to help you make notes from your reading. Don't forget to add the page numbers in case you need to check your notes.

Topic:

Book 1 Title:		Book 2 Title:		Book 3 Title:	
Main fact	Details	Main fact	Details	Main fact	Details